THE QUIET BUTTERFLY
VICTORIA WRIGHT

ISBN 978-1-7364900-8-2

Names: Wright, Victoria (Victoria Ann), author.
Title: The quiet butterfly / Victoria Wright.
Description: [Englewood, Colorado] : Victoria Wright, [2024]] | Includes a list of websites that provide resources for reporting, prevention etc about bullying. | Audience: young adult.
Identifiers: ISBN: 978-1-7364900-8-2 (paperback) | 978-1-7364900-9-9 (ebook)
Subjects: LCSH: Teenage girls--Fiction. | Indigenous youth--Fiction. | Indian women--Fiction. | Bullying in schools--Fiction. | Self-perception in adolescence--Fiction. | Self-actualization (Psychology)--Fiction. | Self-realization--Fiction. | Ethnophilosophy--Fiction. | Traditional ecological knowledge--Fiction. | Indigenous peoples--Poetry. | Indians of North America-- Fiction. | Young adult fiction, American. | LCGFT: Bildungsromans. | BISAC: FICTION / Indigenous. | FICTION / Visionary & Metaphysical.
Classification: LCC: PS3623.R5754 Q54 2024 | DDC: 813/.6--dc23

Library of Congress Control Number: 2024900226

Disclaimer. Neither the author nor the publisher assumes any responsibility for errors or omissions, or contrary interpretations of the subject matter herein. The characters in this book are entirely fictional. Any resemblance to actual persons living or dead is entirely coincidental. Any perceived slight of any individual or organization is purely unintentional.

Cover design by Alexander von Ness
Editing by Donna Mazzitelli
Book Design by Slim Rijeka
Proofreading by Jennifer Bisbing

Printed in United States of America

Published by Victoria Wright
Victoriawright@healingwords.online

Visit www.Healingwords.online

THE
QUIET
BUTTERFLY

VICTORIA WRIGHT

DEDICATION

To the child deep inside.

Butterfly, butterfly, you have many stages of life.
Your wings catch the air as you take flight.
Transforming from egg, larva, pupa to your final birth.
Guide me through the next step of my journey on this earth.

Other Books by Victoria Wright

Healing Words:
To inspire, remember, and know

Listen Within:
A novel of discovery and finding true self

Red, Red, White:
A Novel of True Love and Light

One Deep Breath:
A novel of truth and knowing

Table of Contents

EGG

Female butterflies lay eggs that are no larger than the size of a pin on the host leaf.

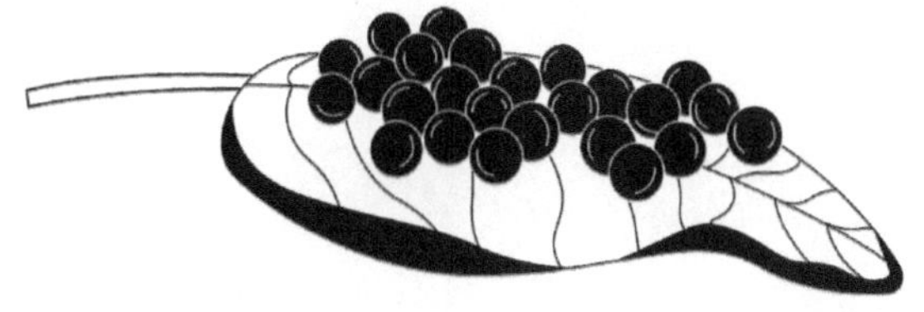

CHAPTER 1

I woke to the shrill of Mom's voice. "Ma, why can't you just let me be? You are never satisfied."

Typically, I'd bury my head in the pillow to drown out the fighting and try to fall back to sleep, but this time it sounded different, serious. Quietly, I slipped out of bed. The creak of the old wooden stairs alerted them to my presence, and they went quiet for a moment. Grandma was in her chair by the window, shaking her head. She loved sitting by the window, giving her a front-row seat to the comings and goings of the neighborhood. Her once-beautiful, thick, black braids that framed her face were now white—a stark contrast to her light brown skin. Over the years, her eyes had dulled, but she was still a stunning Native woman. Grandpa liked to say, "A real looker."

Grandma gazed out the window for what seemed like an eternity, then turned back to Mom. "Mina, I can't do this any-more. I'm tired of fighting. You and Neepa must go." Grand-ma's voice cracked, trying to hold back her emotion.

My heart sank. In my head, I screamed, "NO!" but as usual, nothing came out. They both could see the pain in my eyes. Instead of responding, Mom took a deep breath, looked at me, and said, "Come on, Neepa, let's pack our things." Before leaving the room, Mom said, "Don't worry, Ma, we will be gone in the morning."

Grandma looked so frail sitting in her chair, tears streaming down her face. I desperately wanted to ask her to change her mind, to beg her to let us stay, to assure her that Mom would change and we wouldn't be any trouble. But since Grandpa died, nothing had been the same. More than ever before, Grandma pushed Mom to do more with her life. To stop chasing men and live up to her potential.

Grandpa had never pushed like Grandma. He was softer with Mom, reassuring her that everything would be okay. Grandma thought he was too forgiving, and Grandpa thought she was too tough on Mom, which caused friction between my grandparents. Mom had never liked being told what to do, and with Grandpa gone, the disagreements between Mom and Grandma increased. I could tell Mom missed Grandpa by the lost look in her eyes after she and Grandma argued. We all missed Grandpa. Since he died, I watched my grandmother age before my eyes. I felt it would not be long until she joined him.

Before sunrise, we packed the vintage Jeep Wagoneer with the few belongings we owned and were ready to go. Dented with a few spots of rust, it was the most reliable car Mom had ever owned. It used to be Grandpa's, and he kept it in perfect condition. When he died, it was the only thing he left Mom.

Before Mom could say no, I ran back into the house. There was no way I could leave without saying goodbye to Grandma. She was the most stable person in my life, and I knew this would be the last time I'd see her. Quietly, I opened her bedroom door and knelt beside her bed, taking her once strong and guiding hand that had now become frail in mine and whispered, "I love you." Grandma opened her eyes; tears filled them.

"Neepa, you are an exquisite young lady; you are our beautiful butterfly. Know your grandpa is watching over you. Think of him, and he will come to you if you are frightened, lonely, or just need a friend." She squeezed my hand and slowly repeated, "Know he will always come to you."

"Grandma, I don't want to leave you. Don't make me go," I pleaded.

"Neepa, you must. It will not be long before I join your grandfather. You and your mother need to learn to stand on your own two feet. Your mother needs you, and you need her. Stay strong and know we love you, always have, and always will. Now go, your mother is waiting."

Gently, I kissed Grandma on the forehead. Feeling her soft skin on my lips and looking at her loving face one last time, I seared the moment into my memory and then quietly closed her door behind me. Forcing myself to leave the only place I considered home, I was also leaving the last person who truly saw me. I climbed into the car as Mom quickly wiped a tear from her eye. We drove in silence.

I woke up as the car jerked when we pulled into a diner parking lot. "You awake? It's time to eat."

"Where are we?"

"We just crossed into Iowa."

"Iowa?" I yelled, pushing myself up to see more clearly out the window. "What are we doing here? Mom, where are we going?" I have always hated waking up in the car and realizing we are in another state. If we weren't going back to Chicago, we were moving somewhere else for Mom to find a new job or a new boyfriend.

"Whoa, whoa, slow down. We're heading to Colorado. I thought that would be a good place to start our new lives, plus I have a friend, Josie. She and I worked together in North Dakota when you were young. She's made a good life for herself in Denver as a counselor and has offered to help us out. We can stay with her 'til we get on our feet."

I didn't hide my concern.

"Don't worry, Neepa, it will be okay this time. I promise." I really wanted to believe what Mom said, but if I had a dollar every time I heard that, my last name would be Bezos, not Irving.

Mom and I have always been on the road heading somewhere. Our family was from back east, Massachusetts, but when the government offered a one-way ticket to Chicago for Natives to find work, my grandparents took it, and they never looked back. Like many Natives who moved from their reservation to the city, they lived in the poor part—the red ghetto—which enticed kids to grow up faster than they might have otherwise.

Mom had me at age sixteen, the same age I am now. Who my father is, I don't know; I don't think Mom even knows who he is, either. Due to my unexpected arrival in her life, she didn't finish high school. My grandparents made sure she at least earned her GED, but college was out of the question. It was too bad since my mother is really smart. She has a real knack for numbers, but she chooses to highlight her physique, 36-24-36, versus her intellect, as she believes those numbers will get her a husband. This belief, along with the male attention she's always received, has gotten us into more unfortunate situations than I like to remember. In the end, we'd return to Chicago, my mother's tail between her legs, so she could have time to lick her wounds, pick up the pieces, and for us to start again.

Not knowing anything about my father, the best I can tell is that I got his skin coloring. I like to say I am a coffee with two creams. Apparently, I also got his curls. Mom would pull my hair into two pigtails, creating big cascading curls on each side of my head when I was young. But as I got older, and the bullying began, I chose to wear my hair in a long braid down my back. It hid my curls and made me feel like I actually fit in with all the other Native kids.

Not much has changed. Better to blend in and not be seen or heard. Keeping my clothing simple—T-shirt, jeans, and no makeup—my sole focus now is to get through high school and not end up like my mother.

Sixteen times around the sun, and I've attended eight different schools from Massachusetts to Washington State. Along the way, I picked up the nickname "the quiet girl." No matter where I went or who was talking about me, they always called me the quiet girl. At first, it was deserved because I was painfully shy. A mixed-race kid; people not knowing if I was Native, black, or Asian; then add constantly being the new girl at school, and the name stuck. As I grew older, I did whatever I could to blend in. The less I talked, the easier it was for me to not stick out. To simply disappear into the background. In the end, I grew to like it. It gave me an out to not have to talk. It seemed like every year and every new school, I got quieter and quieter. Now I barely talk to anyone.

Mom grabbed my hand. "Come on, let's get some lunch."

My eyes flashed with surprise.

"Yes, you *have* been asleep for that long."

We walked into the diner and found a booth in the back. It was just like every other diner we had eaten at. There was a long counter with red spinney seats, a glass carousel of pies and cakes, and booths with high backs. The plastic covering on the menu was yellowed and cracked, making it hard to read the handwritten modifications. Nothing looked good, but I knew we wouldn't eat again until we got to Colorado. When the server came to the table, Mom ordered the chicken salad sandwich.

"So, what will you have, honey?" she asked, giving me a warm smile.

I pointed to the cheeseburger and fries on the menu.

She looked at Mom. "She's a pretty thing but a quiet one." Mom smiled and said, "Thank you."

Waiting for the food, I stared out at the parking lot. As cars came and went, my mind drifted to Grandma, and a lump formed in my throat. God, I missed her so much. Sitting at this random roadside diner felt like all the others we had been to: sad and lonely.

Dread began to grow inside me. Another place, another school, no Grandma or Grandpa. How could Grandma do this to me? I loved my mother, but I didn't believe we could make it on our own. We never had to before, at least not for very long. Now we didn't have a safety net. There was a part of me that wanted to be mad at Grandma, to hate her, but how could I hate the person who's always cared for and loved me? Deep down I knew she did this for our own good, but it still hurt. The lump in my throat got bigger. I swallowed hard, pushing the sadness down.

A squirrel pranced across the parking lot. It stopped and looked at me. Mom didn't notice; she was looking at her phone, checking the map to see how many more hours we still had to go.

"Mom, do you see that squirrel?"

"Huh, what?" She looked up.

"The squirrel."

"Oh yeah, what's it doing?"

"I don't know, but doesn't it look like it's watching us?" Before she could answer, it darted off into a tree.

With a full belly back in the car, I slumped down in my seat to try to fall back asleep. Staring off into the empty landscape, my thoughts turned to Grandpa.

"Grandpa, why is the squirrel collecting nuts now? It's summer?" I had asked many years ago.

"They're always collecting, so they will be prepared."

Squirrel, squirrel, you gather like no other.

Making sure there is something for another.

Change may come at any time.

Help me to be prepared with open heart and mind.

"Grandpa, what was that?"

"A poem to help you remember what the squirrel symbolizes. When you see one gathering nuts, remind yourself that change can happen at any time."

That memory of Grandpa made me smile. Maybe this move *will* be different.

Sixteen hours and a few pit stops later, we rolled into Colorado. In all our travels, this was the first time we had been to Denver. Seeing the city skyline on one side of the highway and the majestic mountain range on the other made me feel calmer. The scenery looked so picturesque that it gave me a sliver of hope that everything would be fine. Mom pulled over to the side of the road to call her friend.

"Josie, we made it. We just arrived in Denver." I could hear an excited voice on the other end. "Okay, hold on . . ." Mom looked at me. "Neepa, write this down. 1625 West Leaf Circle. Okay, great. See you soon." She looked at me with a huge smile. "Are you excited? We're about to start our new life."

I gave a half-hearted smile and turned back to stare out the window. Grandpa said change can happen at any time; I just hoped this change would be for the better.

As we drove through the streets, I noticed that the landscape of the neighborhoods had changed from city streets and apartments to manicured lawns, mature trees, and houses set back from the street. Finally, we pulled into the driveway of 1625 W. Leaf Circle. It was a beautiful house, two stories, lots of windows, and a big front lawn. Mom looked in the rearview mirror and smoothed her perfectly straight hair. She lovingly looked over at me, moved a curl from my face, put it around my ear, and gave me a smile, which I knew was to reassure me. Deep down, though, she was asking the same from me.

We walked up to the door, and before we could ring the doorbell, it flew open.

"Mina, it's so good to see you." A tall Native woman with shoulder-length hair and beautiful gray eyes bear-hugged my mother. Seeing Josie next to Mom was an interesting juxtaposition. Mom shapely and Josie tall and lean. Both were gorgeous. What trouble they must have caused. "Neepa, you've grown. It's so very nice to see you again." I averted her look. "Still as quiet as ever, I see."

Mom nodded. "Yes, she is. Josie, I owe you big. Thank you for letting us stay."

"Don't worry, believe me, I know how it is. We have a small apartment downstairs that's not being rented, so you can stay as long as you need to get on your feet. I'll send my son, Enapay, to help you with your stuff." Josie turned and yelled up the stairs.

"Enapay, put your shoes on. We need your help."

A few minutes later, a boy around my age, with thick black hair tied back from his face in a single braid, walked down the stairs. His features were like many of the Native boys I grew up around. However, there was something different about him. He seemed confident and comfortable in his skin; an old soul.

"Enapay, these are my friends Mina and Neepa. Mina and I used to cause trouble back in North Dakota before I met your stepfather," she said with a grin. "They will stay in the apartment for a while."

He looked at both of us with a smile. "Hey, nice to meet you."

I didn't respond.

"So nice to meet you, Enapay, and don't worry, eventually she will talk."

"Why should you? It's not like you are going to be friends," Ego snapped.

I gave my head a good shake to quiet Ego, realizing it had made the trip across country with me. *Here we go again. What do you want now?*

"You know how this works. I'm here to protect you. New place, new people. Things could go south real quick."

We grabbed the stuff from the car and followed Enapay around the back to the apartment entrance. When he opened the door, Mom said, "Holy shit, this place is nice." Josie laughed and turned to me.

"Neepa, does it meet your standards?"

I nodded my head vigorously.

The studio apartment was nicer than any place we had lived before. We walked into the small but nice kitchen. A stove, refrigerator, and bank of cabinets that could hold everything we owned were located against the main wall. Facing the central part of the apartment was a large island that housed the sink, microwave, and, yes, a dishwasher. *Wow, we have never had a dishwasher before!* On the other side of the island was the back of a long bench seat like in fancy restaurants. There was also a small kitchen table and two chairs. The couch was placed against the wall across from the door, and on the far wall was a queen-sized bed with matching bedside tables and a wardrobe.

Separate from the main living space was the bathroom that contained a linen closet, toilet, shower, and sink. Everything looked so new and shiny. I was afraid to touch anything. There were no lingering smells of cigarette smoke or burnt food. It was like no one had lived here before. Even though there was only one window next to the door, it was still bright and airy. The traditional beige or schoolroom green paint colors used in every apartment we'd lived in before was nowhere to be found. Everything was white and seemed to sparkle.

Once everything was brought in from the car, we said our goodnights. Before closing the door, Josie offered to join us the next day to register me at the local high school. It's bad enough to start a new school, but to have to start halfway through the first semester makes it even worse.

"I volunteer at the school all the time, so I have friends over there."

With a look of relief, Mom replied, "That would be great, thank you." She looked at me. "Okay, sweetheart, time for bed. We have a big day tomorrow."

I grabbed my toothbrush and facecloth and went into the bathroom to clean up. When I looked in the mirror, I realized my hair was a disaster, like I had been in a car for almost an entire day. Embarrassment set in. *What did Enapay think?*

"What do you mean, what did he think? He didn't even notice you," Ego so thoughtfully reminded me. *"Why would you think you are worth being noticed?"* Realizing Ego was probably right, the feeling quickly faded. When I came out, Mom had made the bed and was unpacking. Nice. Queen size, so we both would be comfortable. We've slept in smaller.

"Go on, jump in. I'll be in, in just a minute."

When I laid my head on the pillow, it was like I was lying in a cloud. Everything was soft, and it smelled amazing. Already half asleep, I felt Mom slip into bed. She hugged me and whispered in my ear, "Welcome to our new life." I didn't respond. Mom has said that plenty of times before, and so far a new life hasn't meant better.

CHAPTER 2

"Neepa, wake up. We're going to be late." I rolled over to see my mother already dressed, holding a cup of coffee.

"Where did you get that?" I mumbled.

"Josie brought it down. She also dropped off some breakfast. Now come on, we leave in thirty minutes."

I grabbed a muffin and my towel and stumbled into the bathroom. Waiting for the water to get hot, I scarfed down the muffin. *Mm, blueberry.* When I stepped into the shower, it felt amazing. Actual water pressure and the warm water lulled me into a meditative state. *Ahh, I could stay in here all day.* The sound of banging at the bathroom door shocked me back to reality. "Come on, Neepa, let's move it!" Mom yelled.

Stepping out of the shower, I swiped the fog from the mirror and looked at myself. Moving a straggly piece of hair from my face, I thought, *Here we go again. Another school. Maybe this time, our lives will be different. Who am I kidding? It takes more than a beautiful apartment, a comfy bed, and a blueberry muffin for things to be truly different. Mom has a pattern, and I give her three months before she sabotages us again.* Jeans, a clean T-shirt, and my hair tied back in a braid were good enough—no need to work too hard. *There is no guarantee we'll be here that long.*

Just as I was finishing the last of my juice, we heard a car horn. Mom looked over at me. "Well, it's time to go. Josie is driving."

We walked out to the car, and I got in the back. Mom and Josie started right in. Occasionally, a word resonated, but they were catching up on old times and gossiping, so I stared out the window and got lost in my thoughts. When we arrived, it surprised me how large the school looked, bigger than my old school in Chicago. Josie pulled into a visitor parking space and looked back at me.

"Ready for this?"

"Why do they always ask that question?" Ego lamented. *"Don't they know they are just feeding you to the wolves?"* Once again, Ego was right because they always find me.

I gave her a shrug and got out of the car. Mom was quick to jump out. As she did, she grabbed my wrist and, with a stern look, said, "I know we have been through this many times before, but don't take it out on Josie. Remember, she's the one helping us out."

I held the door open for Mom and Josie to enter the school. As Josie walked in, I gave a forced smile and said, "Ready as I'll ever be."

"Yeah right. Excellent cover," Ego remarked.

"Don't worry, Neepa, it's an exceptional school, and you already have one friend. Enapay is in your grade."

"You know he is not going to be your friend. He will pretend to look out for you, but in the end, you are on your own as usual," Ego predicted. *"That's how it has always happened, so why would this*

time be any different?" I shook my head, trying to get Ego to shut up.

Josie guided us to the admissions office. When we walked in, we were welcomed by a lady who didn't look much older than me. Her eyes sparkled with eagerness.

"Hi, how can I help you?"

"Hi, I am Josie Arthur, and my friend here would like to register her daughter."

The lady looked over at us, gave me a smile, and then said, "Just a moment." When she returned, there was a much older man with her.

"Josie, what are you doing in this part of the school? I thought you enjoyed the areas more fun than administration."

"Principal Fern, you know me too well," Josie responded with a heartfelt smile. "My friend has just moved to town, and she would like to enroll her daughter in the eleventh grade."

"Nice." He looked over and gave us both a smile. "My name is Robert Fern, and I'm the principal. Please follow me back to my office, and we can get the paperwork started."

Before we headed back, Josie assured us she would wait there until we were done and then show us around the school. We both gave her an appreciative smile. Mr. Fern was a pleasant-looking man, taller than most, who walked with a slight limp. As he eased himself into his desk chair, he asked, "Do you have any records from your former school?"

I looked at Mom. "No, unfortunately, our move was unexpected, and we weren't able to get Neepa's transcripts," Mom explained.

"Oh, I see. Well, that won't be a problem. We can contact your former school and have them sent over. So, your name is N-e-e-p-a? May I ask its origin?"

Mom responded on my behalf, "We are Native American, Indigenous from back east."

"Wonderful, and I'm sorry, I didn't catch your name."

"Oh, I am Mina Irving, and we just moved from Chicago."

Mr. Fern perked up. "Chicago? White Sox or Cubs fans?"

"Neither. We don't watch baseball," Mom replied.

His enthusiasm faded quickly. "Oh, too bad."

"But my late father would occasionally watch the Cubs," Mom added.

He smiled. "So, Neepa, which high school did you attend in Chicago?" I looked at Mom, and she gave me a reassuring smile.

I lowered my gaze and, looking at my feet, answered, "Purpose High School."

"I'm sorry, I didn't catch that. Can you speak up?"

"OMG, what does he want you to do, yell?" Ego complained.

I shot a glance over at Mom, looking for help. "Neepa is a bit quiet. She said Purpose High School."

"Not too familiar with that school, but we will contact them. To make things easier, why don't you fill out this form, and I'll have our assistant enter you in the system. When you arrive tomorrow, we can get you an identification card and sign you up for classes. Here is our catalog of courses. You will have your mandatory classes, but we have some interesting elective choices as well." He pushed back his chair to get up. "Ladies, I'll leave you to complete the form. When you are done, please return it to Rachel, who you met when you first arrived. Neepa, we're glad you are here, and as the school year progresses, I'm sure you will feel more comfortable and come out of your shell."

Ego laughed. *"I hope he doesn't hold his breath. Remember, the shell is the only thing that protects you. The quieter and more you blend in the better."*

We both looked up at him, nodded, and Mom thanked him before he walked out.

"Well, let's get to it." Mom gestured for me to complete the form. "So, Mr. Fern seemed like a nice man," she mumbled. I rolled my eyes, but she didn't notice since she was on her phone. The form didn't take long to complete. Mom was so engrossed in her mindless scrolling that she didn't even notice that I got up, walked out the door, and was waiting with Josie.

"So, how do you feel?" Josie asked with a smile.

I shrugged my shoulders. "It's just another school."

Mom approached and corrected me. "No, Neepa, this is the last school. I have a good feeling about this place. We're going to make this work." Josie glanced over at me and smiled.

"Ha. We'll see," Ego whispered. *"Just keep a low profile until you move again."*

As promised, Josie gave us a tour of the school. *Wow!* I thought. *Even though the layout is just like the others, this place looks brand new!* If there was one thing I learned from bouncing between schools, most buildings have a similar layout. All I needed was to see the map a few times, and I would know where to go.

On the ride home, I zoned out, letting Mom and Josie continue their gossip session.

"Neepa, Neepa, are you listening?" I looked at Mom as she twisted her head around, trying to look at me. "Did you hear Josie? Look at all these fun shops. She said this is where many of the kids hang out after school." I gave a fake smile, knowing full well that I would not be hanging out here.

"Who is going to invite you to hang out? Do you think you will actually make friends at this school?" Ego remarked. *"I will tell you how this is going to go. Within a week, you will have a target on your back and the bullying will start. You won't say anything because, as we know, it is better to just take it. Mom will get fired, and then you will move again."*

I hated listening to Ego, but most of the time, it was right when it came to Mom.

Lunch was a quick sandwich from a local shop. Mom and Josie planned to focus on finding Mom a job, and I was tasked with doing the unpacking, which I didn't mind since it meant I would have some time alone.

In no time, I finished unpacking the household items. In my box of clothes, I found a shoebox with tape on both sides and my name on top, written in Grandma's handwriting. I gently shook the box; it sounded like papers. Carefully,

I peeled back the tape and lifted the lid. Pictures I hadn't seen before of me as a baby. Pictures of Grandma, Grandpa, and my mom when she was younger. But what caught my eye was an envelope with my name on it in Grandpa's handwriting that was filled with drawings. The drawings were simple but clear, and I could tell that my grandpa drew them. A poem accompanied each drawing. Thumbing through the poems, a small piece of paper fell to the floor. In my grandma's elderly cursive, it said:

"Neepa, I have wanted to share these with you for a long time, but time got away from me. These are the poems that your grandfather would recite to you to help you on your journey of life. Nature is full of wisdom, and he wanted you to open your heart to hear its reminders. If you are feeling lost, listen to nature. It will guide you. Love, Grandma."

I remember when Grandpa would share his poems with me. It was our special time together. *Memories.* As I reminded myself that I needed to hold on to the memories, one came flooding into my mind.

The car slowly pulled into the driveway that we had been to so many times before. The lights were off in the house except for a small glow in the upstairs bedroom. Mom flashed the car headlights a few times, and we waited. Finally, the downstairs light turned on and Grandpa opened the front door. Even at ten years old, I could see the sadness in his eyes. He wasn't sad to see us, but we were not here for a visit. We were back to stay. Mom and I grabbed our stuff and walked into the house.

"Hi, Dad. Thanks for letting us stay." Grandpa hugged Mom and kissed me on the forehead.

"Are you both okay?"

"We are good," Mom answered. Slowly, Grandma came down the stairs. Mom hung her head.

Grandma looked at us. "Neepa, look at how much you've grown over the past year. Are you two hungry?"

Mom looked up. "No, Ma, we ate on the road."

"Okay, well, get your stuff and take it to your room." When I walked past Grandma, she kissed me on the head. She looked at Mom and said, "No need to talk now, we can speak in the morning. Alfred, lock up, and let's all go to bed."

Walking up the stairs, Mom called after me. "Neepa, get ready for bed. I'll be up in just a minute." When I got upstairs, I heard them arguing.

"Mina, I said we can talk in the morning. No need to get everyone in a tizzy tonight. Go to bed, it looks like you had a long day." I could hear Grandma climb the stairs, and as she passed our room, she poked her head in. "It's good to see you, Neepa, I missed you."

"I missed you, too, Grandma. Goodnight."

I woke to the wonderful smell of pancakes and bacon. It was so good to be back. Grandma and Grandpa always took good care of me. They made me feel like I was home. I ran down the stairs and gave them both big hugs and kisses. Mom wasn't up yet, so we talked quietly. When she finally came down, I had already finished my breakfast. Mom instructed me to get ready because we needed to get me registered back at school. Which also meant they needed time to talk, so I didn't rush.

"Mina, it sounded like everything was going so well. It was a good-paying job. What happened?" Grandma asked.

"Yeah, well, it was 'til it wasn't. Someone from the tribe thought that I looked at their man the wrong way, so we were out."

"Oh, Mina."

"Ma, it's not like it's my fault. Plus, it takes two to tango. All I did was smile. You know how it is. I may be Native, but they'll take the side of their tribal member over mine."

"That's okay, honey. Stay here for a while and get back on your feet. I know you will find something soon," Grandpa reassured.

"Thanks, Dad."

"So how is Neepa? She's so sensitive. How's she holding up?" Grandpa asked.

"Well, I know she's happy to be back. The girls at her school out there were not nice, and with her being so quiet and all, she got bullied."

"Mina, you need to protect her," Grandma scolded.

"Ma, I tried, but I was also trying to protect my job so we could eat. Neepa needs to learn to speak up. She's going to have to learn how to protect herself."

"Keep your voice down, she doesn't need to hear this," Grandma instructed. "You know as well as we do that that is not what she is about. Neepa sees and feels things that many of us can't. Her energy is strong, and she has the gift of knowing. Once she realizes it and trusts it, she will be very powerful and will help many.

"I know, Ma."

"Why is she always getting bullied? Can't the school do anything?"

"When she tells me, I go to the school and complain, but it doesn't stop. She's getting older now, so she needs to figure something out because I can't be there all the time to protect her. She needs to stand up for herself and be strong."

Before coming down the stairs, I made a loud noise so they could stop talking about me.

"Hi, honey, you ready?" Mom asked.

I nodded my head. "Alright, give me ten, and I'll be ready to go."

Grandpa looked at me with a twinkle in his eyes. "Neepa, when you come back, would you like to take a walk in the park with me? I've missed having my walking buddy." An enormous smile grew on my face. "I'll take that as a yes then." He laughed.

When Mom and I walked out the door, I could hear Grandma and Grandpa arguing.

"Clara, why are you so hard on Mina? She's doing her best."

"Alfred, I know she has been having a hard time, but we're not going to be around forever. Mina needs to get her act together so she can stand on her own two feet. As much as Neepa needs to stand up for herself, Mina needs to get her priorities straight. If she doesn't, I'm afraid to think of what will happen when we're no longer here."

Grandpa was waiting on the front stoop when we returned. "Ready, Butterfly?" he asked, wearing a warm grin. I nodded my head. "So how was school?" Grandpa asked after we had been walking for a few minutes. I shrugged.

"Grandpa, why do you call me butterfly?"

"Because, just like a butterfly, you have many stages in your life, each one transforming you. When you are ready, you will take flight and grace this world with your magnificence and beauty. Plus, did you know that butterflies have two hearts? They're filled with love, just like you are."

"Two hearts?"

"Yes, my butterfly." Something caught Grandpa's attention. "Oh, Neepa, do you see that hummingbird? Look at how wonderful it is."

The hummingbird darted back and forth in front of us, just begging to be seen. "Do you know what the hummingbird is telling you?"

I gave Grandpa a puzzled look.

"Neepa, nature always has messages for us, and if we are open to receiving them, they can help guide us on this journey we call life. Look at it, what do you think it's trying to tell you?"

I watched it as it dipped its beak into a flower. "Joy," I answered.

"Why would you say that?"

"Because it brings me joy watching it."

"Yes, it is reminding you to see the joy in life." Grandpa gave me a smile and then recited:

Hummingbird, hummingbird, your vibration is pure delight.

Darting here and there is magic in flight.

Sharing your beauty and love to remove life's strife.

Open my heart so I may taste the nectar of this life.

Whenever you see an animal or creepy crawly, always ask yourself if they are bringing a message for you. You will know."

"But, Grandpa, how will I know what the message is?"

"Our people followed nature closely and listened to the messages they had for us. If you have a question, you can always ask me, but like you just did, deep down you know the answer. The hummingbird brings you joy, and it wanted to remind you to see more joy."

"Grandpa?"

"Yes, what is it?" He saw the worry on my face. "What is wrong?"

"What if I cannot see joy?"

"Neepa, I know you have had a hard time, always moving, new schools. It can be hard for a kid. Heck, it would be hard for an adult. But you must release the negative and open yourself to the positive."

"How do I do that, Grandpa?"

"Quiet down your head and live through your heart." He could see the confusion in my eyes. He brought me over to a bench, and we sat down. "Neepa, your ego limits you. This may sound crazy, but do you ever hear a voice inside your head that says you can't do something or tells you other negative messages like that?"

I looked down. "Yes. Is that normal?"

"Yes. It's called your ego. It's nothing to be ashamed of. We all have one. It's there to protect us and to keep us comfortable. When we do something different or are in an uncomfortable position, Ego will come on strong. The problem occurs when it rules our lives, limiting our dreams and making us believe we can't do anything. When that happens, it is time to quiet it down."

"But how?"

"By listening to your heart. Doing the things that bring you joy. Challenging yourself or stepping out of your comfort zone to grow. Remember, your heart tells you that you can. Ego tells you that you can't."

"Grandpa, I hear Ego a lot."

"I know. But remember, just because things happened a certain way in the past, does not mean they will happen the same way in the future. You have a choice to listen to either your ego or your heart. The more you listen to your heart, the happier you will be."

"Grandpa, you always tell me I can, so you must be my heart." Grandpa grabbed my hand and gave it a squeeze. "Neepa, you certainly are my heart."

Wiping a tear from my eye. I thought, *Grandpa, I wish we could walk in the park just one more time.*

CHAPTER 3

I heard Mom's footsteps coming closer to the front door, so I grabbed the box and put it under the bed until I could find a better hiding place.

"Wow, you do good work," Mom complimented as she looked around, noticing everything had a place. Josie and I are going food shopping. Do you want to come?"

I shook my head and showed her the course catalog as if to remind her that I needed to pick my classes.

"Okay, suit yourself. We shouldn't be long. Enapay will be home soon from school, and Josie asked that he come down and visit so he can tell you all about the high school blah, blah, blah." Before she closed the door on her way out, she popped her head back in. "Neepa, honey, I know you are sad and miss Grandma. Believe it or not, I miss her as well, but it was time we stood on our own feet. Give me a chance to prove that this is going to work out. Please, just give me and all of this a chance." She blew me a kiss before closing the door.

Knowing that I had at least an hour before she returned, I made myself comfortable on the couch and leisurely flipped through the pages of the course catalog. Mr. Fern said there were some good electives, but it all looked pretty run-of-the-mill to me. I put down the catalog and closed my eyes. The next thing I knew, Enapay was sitting at the kitchen table looking at me.

"Hey, cuz," he said casually.

I jumped up, throwing the catalog and nearly missing his head.

"Hey, watch out!"

"Well, don't sneak up on a sleeping person like that."

"Be careful of him, Neepa. Remember, we can't trust anyone," Ego reminded me.

"Oh, so she can speak. Good to know." I glared as I walked past him to pick up the catalog. "So, my mom asked that I come down and tell you about school. What do you want to know?"

"It wasn't me who asked, and why are you calling me cuz? I'm not your relative."

"Nice comeback," Ego complimented.

"Snippy, snippy. I like you better when you are quiet. You'll find out that there aren't many of us around here, so the ones that are here, we become family. Plus, we're all related anyway, right?" He paused, letting me digest what he just said. "So, why are you here in Colorado? What was so bad about Chicago? Too cold?" He laughed.

In a low scratchy voice, I said, "My grandma kicked us out." I tried to clear my throat, but it was too dry. Walking into the kitchen, I grabbed a glass of water. Since we arrived in Colorado, I'd been thirsty. Mom said it was due to the elevation. That's why they call Denver the Mile High City. It is literally a mile high from sea level.

"Ouch. That sucks," he said, as he watched me guzzle my glass of water. "And don't worry, I wasn't thirsty." We sat in silence for a few minutes. "Well, since you don't talk much, I'll tell you what I know. You can take it or leave it." Enapay proceeded to tell me about his classes, which teachers were good and which ones to stay away from. He outlined the usual clique structure that every school had and informed me that a lot of these kids were rich, so they drive themselves to school.

I looked at him and asked, "So how did you guys get here?"

"My mom met my stepdad when we were back in North Dakota. I was like five when they married, and we moved here to Colorado. He died two years ago, so it's just me and my mom again."

I lowered my eyes. "Sorry for your loss."

"No need to be sorry. It wasn't your fault. Freak plane accident. None of us expected it. Well, I gotta go. Homework." I nodded. "Pick you up tomorrow at eight-fifteen sharp to catch the bus, and don't worry, I won't cramp your style." He laughed as he walked out.

Not long after Enapay left, I heard Mom coming toward the door. I ran to open it, and she shoved two bags into my arms. "There are three more bags in the trunk. Go get them, please. I gotta pee." She pushed past me and beelined it to the bathroom. I put the bags on the table and went out to get the rest. Josie was gathering the last of her bags as I walked to the car. She smiled. "So, did Enapay help you out?"

I nodded my head, "Yes, he did. Thanks."

"Neepa, I know you and your mom have had some hard times, and I know this seems like just another stop, but your mom really wants to make this a home for you and her. She's under a lot of pressure to get this right, so just give her a chance. Moms aren't always perfect, even though we may try."

I nodded my head, acknowledging that I would give Mom a chance. Before walking away, I turned back to Josie. "I am sorry for your loss."

"Thank you, Neepa. That means a lot to me."

"Neepa, you ready? We can't miss the bus," I heard Enapay yelling out and banging on the door. I grabbed my bag and a snack from the counter, then kissed Mom quickly, and closed the door behind me. Walking up the driveway, he looked at me. "So, you ready?"

"Why does everyone ask me that question? It's not like this is my first rodeo."

"Yeah, but this place is not Chicago. These kids can be pretty pretentious. I told you they have money." I rolled my eyes. "Oh, and you will want to learn how to speak up." I glared at him. "I'm just saying kids can be mean. So, it's better to be mean first than to be a pushover. They already think we're quiet and humble. Don't perpetuate the stereotype."

There were about ten kids waiting for the bus. Each one eyed me up and down. To avoid their looks, I kept my eyes down.

"Oh great, here we go again," Ego bemoaned.

Once the bus arrived, everyone looked up from their phones and lumbered up the stairs. I got on before Enapay and found an empty seat. As he approached, he asked, "Do you want me to sit with you? Don't want to cramp your style." I shrugged.

"Boy, he's pushy," Ego noted.

He motioned for me to slide over and sat down next to me anyway. I stole a quick side glance at Enapay.

"Yes, he may be cute, but don't even think about it," Ego was quick to remind me. The rest of the bus ride, I just looked straight ahead. When we arrived, Enapay looked relieved.

Walking off the bus, it seemed like we stepped into pure chaos. Kids and teachers going in every direction. Enapay hit my arm. "This way." I followed him, and we ended up at the admissions office. He nudged me. "Go on, this is where you pick up your identification card. And hurry up. I don't want to be late."

Walking into the office, I immediately recognized the woman Rachel from the day before. She greeted me with a smile.

"Neepa, isn't it?" I smiled back. "Okay, here you go. ID card, laptop, and your mandatory classes, plus a map. Have you picked an elective yet?"

"Uh, no."

"Well, do that before the end of the day and come back to let me know. I need to make sure there is room for you."

"Okay. Oh and thanks," I said under my breath. When I walked out, Enapay looked like a kid at Christmas.

"So, what classes did you get?" I handed him the paper. "Okay, we have geometry and biology together. Yikes, you have Ms. Jones for history. Good luck with that. But at least you have Mr. Wright for English. Wait, you're in AP English?" He looked at his phone. "Oh shit, we're going to be late. I'll drop you off at your first class." We ran down the hall, and he gestured to a room. "I'll see you in biology," he yelled.

When I pushed open the door, everyone looked, expecting it to be the teacher. My arrival caused a stir, and the entire class erupted in whispers. I found a seat in the back. Not a minute after the teacher entered, I heard someone say, "There's a new kid in the back."

Mr. Wright looked around, and our eyes locked. He waved me up to his desk. "Good morning, Miss . . . ?"

"Um, Neepa. Neepa Irving."

"Nice to meet you. I am Mr. Wright, and this is AP English. Is this where you are supposed to be?"

I looked at the paper. "Yes, I'm in your class."

"Okay, great, and welcome." Mr. Wright stood. "Everyone, I'd like to introduce you to our new student, Neepa Irving. She joins us from . . ." he looked at me.

"Chicago," I croaked. Everyone laughed.

"Excuse me, let's have some manners," Mr. Wright reminded everyone. "Well, it is nice to have you. We're just finishing up *Animal Farm* by George Orwell, so you came at a good time. Sit back and enjoy the discussion."

"Thank you," I murmured.

"*Nice job, you dweeb. Now everyone is going to tease you for croaking,*" Ego projected.

To ignore Ego, I paid close attention to everyone in the class to understand what I was up against. No one really stuck out, but they could tell I was studying them. One of the many benefits of not talking much is you notice a lot more about people than you would otherwise. Class went by surprisingly fast. When the bell rang, Mr. Wright called me to his desk and handed me a book.

"Miss Irving, the next book we will be reading is *Heart of Darkness*. Have you read this one yet?"

"Yes."

"Well, you will be ahead of the class then. I'll look to you to help explain some of the more advanced themes."

Fear washed over me.

"Are you okay?" Mr. Wright asked.

Lowering my head, I mumbled, "I don't like to speak in front of people."

"Understood, but that is something you'll need to work on. Everyone speaks in my class. What is your next class?"

I reviewed my schedule. "Biology with Ms. White."

"Two doors down on your left. Have a good day, Miss Irving."

When I entered biology, I heard a boy say in a croaky voice, "Well, isn't it Miss Chicago?" I walked to the back of the room and sat at an empty table.

"*See, I told you so*," Ego pointed out.

Enapay got up from his seat and joined me. "What was that about? Already making friends, I see." I rolled my eyes. When Ms. White began class, she looked around the room and spotted me.

"Neepa Irving, glad you could join us. We have lab today, so I hope you are familiar with dissecting." I looked at her and nodded. "I also see you have a lab partner. Wonderful, and thank you, Enapay, for welcoming Neepa to eleventh grade biology." A few kids snickered, but they quickly stopped when Ms. White looked in their direction.

Lunch couldn't come fast enough. Enapay and I headed to the cafeteria.

"Did you bring something? Because I have to buy."

I nodded.

"Are you okay sitting by yourself?"

I rolled my eyes.

"Fine, I was just trying to be nice."

When Enapay walked away, I found an empty table and waited for him to return. I could feel everyone looking at me, so I pulled a book from my bag and read while I waited. When I looked up to locate Enapay, I noticed two girls coming my way. I put my head down quickly, pretending to read.

"*Shit, shit, shit*," Ego squealed.

"Hi, Neepa?" I looked up. "My name is Julie, and this is Rebecca. We're Enapay's friends. He said he'll be right over. Do you mind if we join you?" I shook my head.

"So, how do you like the school so far?" Rebecca asked.

"It's okay," I responded. Just then, Enapay joined us. He looked at them.

"Don't worry, she's not a big talker; I'm surprised she said anything to you. Now she's going to shoot me a dirty look. That's how we communicate," he said with a smile.

"Enapay, that's rude. Not everyone is as talkative as you," Rebecca replied. I giggled.

"*She's funny. We could like her*," Ego noted.

"Oh, you like that one, huh?" Enapay looked at me.

I sat and listened as they chatted about the day. Just as we were getting up to leave, a group of guys passed by and in unison said Chicago in croaky voices. The three of them looked at me. Julie yelled out "piss off" and then they replied in unison with a round of, "Ooh, we're scared!"

"Seriously, Neepa, what is that about?" Enapay asked.

"It's nothing," I mumbled.

"Alright," he responded, shaking his head.

We all went separate ways, but before Enapay left, he asked, "Do you know where you are going?"

I looked at the map and nodded my head.

"K. See you in geometry."

Since I didn't have an elective, I found my way to the library to wait until my next class. The library seemed new, pristine almost, and there weren't too many kids inside. At my old school, the library had a distinct smell of old books mixed with the librarian's lunch. I wandered through the stacks, running my finger across the books. The library was always my safe place when things got bad at my other schools.

Placed at the end of one row was a small table. I made myself comfortable and pulled out the course catalog. Art, technology, Spanish, French, Mandarin, drama, choir, band, visual arts. It was the same selection as my old school. Languages were not my thing, so I took those out of the equation. Not caring about the other electives, I closed my eyes and ran my finger down the list. It landed on visual arts. Well, I guess that's my new elective, I said to myself. There were still thirty minutes before my next class, so I gathered my stuff and headed to the admissions office. Not more than a few minutes after exiting the library door, a teacher stopped me in the hall.

"Excuse me, what are you doing out of class?" he asked sternly.

"Um, I'm new, and I don't have an elective. I was heading to admissions to pick one."

"New, huh, let me see your ID." I handed it over to him. He took it and started walking.

"Oh, now you are in trouble," Ego teased.

"Hey, hey, what are you doing?" I called after him and ran to catch up.

He turned and looked at me. "I'm escorting you to admissions. Students cannot be outside of class without a pass." When we got to admissions, he opened the door for me. "Hi Rachel, I see we have a new student." He looked at my ID and slowly read, "N-e-e-p-a Irving."

"Yes, Bill, we do. Is there a problem?"

"No, I just found her in the hall without a pass. She said she needs to register for an elective."

"Yes, she does. Neepa, have you made your decision?"

"Visual arts," I whispered.

"I'm sorry, I didn't catch that. What did you say?"

I cleared my voice. "Visual arts."

"Great choice," she responded, checking her computer. "And you are in luck. There is room. I'll add you to the class roster. You still have some time before the next period. You can wait here if you like."

I nodded.

"Alright then, I'll leave you in Rachel's capable hands," Bill announced and handed me my ID. "Nice to meet you, Neepa, and I hope the next time we meet, you will have a hall pass."

Once the door closed, she looked at me. "Sorry about that. Mr. Anderson takes his job seriously." I smiled. "Do you need anything else?"

"A locker."

"Oh, of course. Sorry about that." Rachel put her head down and began frantically clicking her keyboard. "Okay, your locker is 528, and here is your lock." She turned and headed to the printer then handed me my final schedule. "So, everything going well so far?"

"Sort of," I uttered.

"Oh no. That doesn't sound good. I hope the other students are being nice."

I was about to answer, but then the office door swung open. In a croaky voice, I heard, "Chicago, don't tell me you are already in trouble on your first day."

Rachel butted in. "Michael, is there something you need?"

"Oh yeah. The principal said he would write me a recommendation, so I wanted to see if it was ready."

Rachel checked the outgoing bin. "Doesn't look like it. Why don't you try back tomorrow."

"Sure thing. It's always nice to see you, Rachel." Michael looked back at me. "See you, Chicago."

When the door closed, she looked at me and knew what was going on. "Don't pay any attention to him. He is all noise."

I nodded my head but knew he would be a thorn in my side.

The rest of the day sailed by. Calculus and history were uneventful, and everyone stared as usual. However, there was a group of girls that gave me the stink eye in the hall. Also not unusual, so I just kept my head down and walked past. When I got home, there was a note from Mom on the table.

"Neepa, I'm out looking for a job. Will be home by six. Please make dinner. Love you."

That gave me a couple of hours to be alone. Exhausted from meeting so many people, I needed to decompress. A snack and the couch were calling my name.

Staring off into space, sadness overwhelmed me. If we were back in Chicago, I would have told Grandma about my day. It was easier speaking with Grandma and Grandpa than anyone else. They understood me, and there were times when all we did was sit in silence. Thinking about Grandma, I reached under the bed and pulled out the box of pictures and her note. My body ached to feel her hug. Tears started slowly then they came gushing out like a busted water pipe. Loneliness filled me. Curled into the fetal position, I muffled my cries with my shirt. After a few moments, I pulled myself together and decided a scenery change would help me.

The neighborhood was still unfamiliar, so I only dared to take a short walk around the block. The fresh air was supposed to make me feel better, but seeing all the expensive houses made me feel even more out of place.

"Are you sure you are supposed to be here? Someone is going to ask what you are doing in this neighborhood," Ego warned.

Luckily, I stumbled upon a small greenbelt kind of park. This felt more comfortable. There was not a lot of activity, so I plopped down on a small bench. Occasionally, someone passed by walking their dog, but otherwise, it was quiet. From the corner of my eye, a beautiful green hummingbird caught my attention, darting around like it was dancing for me. A warm feeling of happiness filled me and lightened my mood. When it made its last pass, I realized it was getting late, and I needed to make dinner.

Mom was not a skilled cook and believed we could make everything from a box or can, so fresh wasn't in her vocabulary. Luckily, Grandma thought it was important that I learn to cook at a very early age, so it was now my responsibility. Once home, I rifled through the cupboard and found egg noodles, grabbed some frozen peas, and decided on baked chicken.

Mom came home like a tornado. "Hi, honey. How was your day?"

Before I could even answer, she started telling me about hers and how she applied for jobs at a medical office, two retail stores, and as a front office person for a major architectural firm. I smiled as she rambled on and on. Finally, when she stopped to take a breath, she said, "Mm, dinner smells great. What are we having?" Just at that moment, I pulled the chicken out of the oven. "Oh, chicken. Looks great, honey. Let me wash up, and I'll set the table." When we sat down to eat, Mom was still buzzing. "So, I'm sorry, honey. Did you tell me about your day?"

"It was okay," I replied. "Same old, same old."

"Did Enapay help you out? Josie asked that he look out for you."

"Um, hmm."

"Well good. It's always nice to see a friendly face among the masses. Did you make any friends?"

My twisted facial expression should have explained it, but just to be sure, I said, "No."

"Seriously, did she say friends? Does she know you?" Ego butted in.

"Well, if you didn't make friends, did you make any enemies?"

I looked down and was quiet.

"Neepa, what happened?"

"Nothing important."

She gave me the eye, so I knew I had to give her more. "Fine. In my first class, my voice made a funny croaking noise when I said we moved from Chicago. Now there's a guy who keeps on calling me Chicago in a croaky voice. It's not like I made an enemy, he is just bothersome."

"Honey, he is trying to get your attention. You are a beautiful girl."

I looked away and under my breath said, "I doubt that." To me, high school kids are classified into eight semi-exclusive groups. Popular, athletes, artsy, smart, gamers, bullies, LMAs (leave me alone), and others. I was considered "other," and he looked like an athlete. The two don't mix. Mom looked at me.

"Don't be surprised. The male species thinks differently than us."

I rolled my eyes.

She continued the questioning. "Did you meet any nice girls?"

"There were a couple of girls that Enapay is friends with that were nice."

"You know I always have to ask. Did you meet any mean girls?"

I tried to look away again, but that didn't work.

"Neepa?"

"I don't know if they're mean, but I got the stink eye from a group of them in the hall."

Mom let out an enormous sigh. "I'm sorry, honey. Sometimes the female species isn't much better. Please know it is jealousy. They don't know you from Adam, so all they see is a beautiful girl, which means more competition. Please, honey, just watch your back."

I nodded, knowing full well that they could cause me real problems.

"Enough of that stuff. After dinner, let's take a ride around town, just so that we can get our bearings?"

My Cheshire smile said it all.

After the drive, exhaustion hit hard. Mom was tired as well. We cleaned up and collapsed into bed. Before Mom slipped into deep sleep, I whispered, "I love you." Since coming to Denver, Mom's attitude had been different. Maybe she was really trying to make this a better life for us, or maybe she was just as scared as I was, so this time it had to work. Mom squeezed my arm and was out. It took me a bit longer to quiet my mind. All I could think about was how much I missed Grandma and Grandpa. Finally, I drifted off to sleep.

"Neepa, my little butterfly, wake up." Slowly, I opened my eyes, and standing in the distance was Grandpa. But we weren't in the apartment; we were out in the forest. I ran to Grandpa and gave him a big hug. "Oh, Grandpa, I missed you so much."

"I know, but I'm always with you. Whenever you need me, I am with you."

"Where are we?"

"We are in your soul. This is where you will find me, right here within you." I was confused, but it didn't matter. I was with Grandpa.

"So, kiddo, you've been having a bit of a rough patch."

"Grandpa, honestly, we have been much worse off, but I'm afraid . . ."

"Of what?"

"That I will like this new life too much and then we'll have to leave again. If that happens, we have no place to go."

"Please do not worry. It all works out the way it should. But you must live your life without worrying about what *may* happen. You can't forget the beauty of life. Remember when you were younger and we saw the hummingbird in the park, and I asked you how it made you feel?"

"Yes."

"The hummingbird was there to remind you to see the beauty in life, and when that happens, it removes life's strife. Like the hummingbird, drink the nectar of this sweet life."

Looking at Grandpa and the twinkle he had in his eyes, I knew he was the hummingbird that I had seen in the park earlier. "Thank you, Grandpa." Slowly, his image faded. I yelled out, "Grandpa, please don't leave me. Don't go."

"Neepa, Neepa, honey, are you okay?"

I woke up to Mom shaking me. At that moment, I realized it was all a dream.

CHAPTER 4

After my first week of school, I fell into a routine: sleep, eat, bus, classes, eat, homework, sleep. Rinse and repeat. Enapay and his friends helped me feel more comfortable. Julie and Rebecca were funny. They kept Enapay in line. On the bus ride to school, I asked Enapay why he only hung out with girls.

"Have you met the guys who go to school here? I'm tired of being called chief or being asked why I wear my hair like a girl. They're stupid, and I don't need to waste my time trying to change people who I know won't change. Girls are smarter, and Rebecca and Julie get me. Plus, Rebecca grew up around Natives down in New Mexico, so she gets my humor."

I nodded my head in agreement, at the same time trying to hide my envy that he could make such good friends. As soon as we got to school, I was quickly reminded that not all girls were nice and that I still had the issue with those girls who gave me the stink eye.

Unfortunately for me, they congregated a few feet from my locker, making sure I would see them often. When I asked Enapay who they were, all he said was, "They're not the type of girls you want to make enemies with." Great, it seemed like they had already made that decision for me. My locker wasn't conveniently located, and not having a lot of time in between classes, I only went there a few times a day.

The day came when *those girls* decided to "introduce" themselves. Just as I closed my locker, I felt a strange sensation. The hairs on the back of my neck prickled and then I heard, "Hey, hey you, what's your name?"

"*Neepa, move it,*" Ego warned.

This felt all too familiar. I was hopeful this place would be different, but hope didn't change the inevitable. Trying to avoid looking at them, I turned and started walking down the hall. The next thing I knew, my back slammed against the lockers. My eyes closed as I winced in pain. When I opened them, the biggest of them was right in my face.

"Didn't you hear me? What's your name?" she overpronunciated to make sure if I didn't hear her, I could read her lips.

I looked down and mumbled, "Neepa."

"N-e-e what? I can't hear you?"

Again, I mumbled, "Neepa."

She turned to her *girls* in a sickly sweet voice and announced, "Oh, she's a quiet girl."

The bell rang, which saved my ass, but before they left, one of them knocked my notebooks out of my arms. Running down the hall, they all yelled, "See you, Quiet Girl." I tried to collect my belongings as quickly as I could. When I got up, Michael was standing in front of me and handed me one of my books.

"Here you go, Chicago." But before he left, he warned, "Be careful."

I pulled myself together and got to history class. Ms. Jones locked her door after the bell, requiring late students to knock to be allowed in. I knocked once. She looked at me, glanced at her watch, then opened it. "Miss Irving, since you are new, I won't hold this against you, but my rule is, first late, you get a warning. Second, detention, and third, you are removed from my class. Understood?"

"Yes."

"Good, now take your seat."

Before I sat down, someone said, "What happened? Did you drop your books?"

"Miss Lawrence, did you have something to say?" the teacher asked.

"No, Ms. Jones."

Wonderful, it was one of them. How did I not notice her before? I stared at her and could feel her nervousness. She looked back at me and then quickly turned away.

Enapay was the first person I saw when I got to calculus class. He mouthed, "Are you okay?"

Nodding my head, I thought, *Wow, word travels fast.*

On the bus ride home, I was quieter than usual, which meant dead silent. Enapay tried to make small talk, but it was clear I was not interested. Luckily, Mom wasn't home when I arrived, giving me time to calm down and do my homework. When she arrived later, her energy was low. Changing from her interview clothes into grubbies, she sat at the table. "So, how was your day?"

"Okay."

"Nothing eventful happened?"

I paused. *"Don't do it. Keep your mouth shut,"* Ego instructed.

"Nope."

"Well, that's good, right?"

I smiled, hoping she believed me. "How was your day? Any leads?"

"I filled out several applications. If I don't hear by next week, there is a temp agency that I can go to and hopefully find something through them." I could feel Mom's eyes on me, and she could tell I was feeling down.

"Hey, Neepa, I was thinking you haven't spoken to Grandma since we arrived in Denver. Would you like to—

"Yes!" I shouted before Mom could finish her question.

"Okay, okay, not too long, though. I need to save my minutes." Mom handed me her phone.

"Got it." I was dialing Grandma's number before I could close the bathroom door. It rang several times, but I knew I had to give her time to get up and get to the phone. Finally, she picked up.

"Hello?"

"Hi, Grandma, it's Neepa."

"Oh, Neepa, how are you?"

"I'm good. We both are. How are you doing?"

"Good." There was a long pause. "Just a bit slower. So, tell me everything."

I didn't have much time, so I got to the important stuff. "Grandpa came to me in my dream."

"Oh, Neepa, that is wonderful. He will come in your dreams when you quiet your mind and when you think of him. Have you made friends yet?"

"Sort of."

"Is anyone bothering you?"

My silence spoke volumes. "Neepa, you are getting older now, and it is time for you to speak up. For a long time, our oppressors wanted to keep us silent. They called us stoic, but they had beaten us down for so long that it was just easier to say nothing. Your ancestors who walk with your grandfather now fought hard to have their voice heard, to be counted. Do not waste their efforts. Stand up for yourself, and let people know who you are. You are too special to hide. Be strong, my butterfly. Look for the chameleon poem, it should help."

"When you talk to Mom, please don't tell her. She has enough to worry about; I'll figure this out myself."

Grandma reluctantly agreed. "I love you, Neepa, and tell your mother I love her too."

"I love you too, Grandma." Hanging up the phone made me sad. In the pit of my stomach, I knew there was only a short amount of time that Grandma had left on this earth before she would be with Grandpa. Swallowing the lump that had formed in my throat, I looked in the mirror and heard her voice again. "Be strong, my butterfly."

Mom was making something out of a box for dinner when I handed her the phone. I hugged her and told her that Grandma said she loved her. Mom tried to hide her emotions. "I'm cooking here, don't interrupt the chef," she said then shooed me away. After dinner, Mom jumped in the shower, giving me some time to look for the poem.

Chameleon, chameleon, you hide so well.

Danger is something you can foretell.

Sensitivity and clairvoyance are your psychic gifts.

Show me so I may know when to shift.

That night, I had a vivid dream of a chameleon. Its eyes looked in different directions at the same time, seeing everything around it. I watched as it blended into its surroundings then within moments it changed its colors to stand out. If only I could be like a chameleon.

To ensure that what happened the day before did not happen again, I asked Enapay to be with me while I emptied my locker. Rather than worrying about being beaten up every day, I decided to carry all my stuff with me. At lunchtime, it felt like my first day all over again. Whispers and stares. When Enapay, Rebecca, and Julie sat down, they asked what was going on. Shrugging my shoulders, I indicated I had no idea. Two girls passed our table. One said to the other, "Did you see what they did to the quiet girl? It's blowing up all over the internet."

We all looked at each other. Rebecca got up and went over to another table to find out what was going on. Sitting back down, her face looked uneasy. "Someone took a video of T pushing Neepa into the lockers. The video is all over the place."

Enapay looked at me. "You okay, cuz?"

I nodded my head and said, "Doesn't matter to me. I don't have a phone, and I already know what happened." None of them thought my humor was funny. "Why do they call her T?" I asked.

"Her real name is Tamara, but she doesn't like it. The only people who can get away with calling her that are the teachers. I'm sorry you are her target. There is always one kid she doesn't like and then torments them for the rest of the year," Julie explained.

"Guess I'm just lucky like that."

They laughed, but I could tell they were concerned. Rebecca's face turned serious. "Hey, Neepa, why don't you tell a teacher? You don't want this to blow up."

I shook my head. "That will just make it worse."

By the time calculus came, I was done, tired of people whispering and calling me "quiet girl." Walking in, I noticed a very tall man writing on the whiteboard. The regular teacher had been on sick leave, so I hadn't met him yet. Looking over to Enapay, I eye motioned to the teacher, and he nodded, as if to say this is the real one. Before I sat down, there was a tap on my shoulder. Turning around, I found myself face to chest with him. He looked down at me. "Neepa Irving, I believe." My eyes went from the bottom of his chest and traveled up to see his handsome face. Feeling like a little kid, all I could say was, "Uh-huh."

"I'm Mr. Ellison. It's nice to meet you, and welcome to calculus. Apologies that this is the first time meeting you. I have been out on sick leave." I just stared. "Are you getting settled?"

I nodded.

"Well, I can see you are a woman of few words. Please know I'm always here if you need any help."

I smiled, quickly turned, and sat in my seat. Looking over at Enapay, he could hardly contain himself. Lowering my head to hide my smile, I laughed at myself as well. I probably looked like a little girl standing next to him.

Outside of the T incident, life was going pretty well for me. Classes were good, with no real catchup from changing schools. Enapay, Julie, and Rebecca were becoming my friends, and I stayed out of the crosshairs of T and her crew. When I got home, there was a note on the table from Mom. "Clean up and look nice. We're going out for dinner. Pick you up at six o'clock." *Sounds like Mom got a job.*

Looking nice was easier said than done. All I had were jeans and T-shirts, oh and one sweater, so I decided that was what I would be wearing. At six o'clock on the dot, I met

Mom outside. Before I could open the car door, she commented through the passenger side window, "Aren't you going to be warm in that sweater?"

"You said look nice, and this is all that I had."

"Go back into the house and grab one of my blouses. Hurry, we don't want to be late."

I did as I was told and put on a nice blue printed shirt. Getting back into the car, Mom said, "Wow, look at you. You look great in that shirt. My baby looks all grown up."

I blushed. Trying to make some room in the shirt, I started pulling at it.

"Neepa, what are you doing? Is there something wrong?"

"Mom, it's too tight. I feel like I'm wearing a straitjacket."

"Honey, this is not one of your oversized T-shirts. It's a fitted shirt."

To make sure Mom wouldn't get mad at me, I stopped squirming, but I felt really self-conscious.

"Geez, Neepa, are you gaining weight? Why are the girls so big?" Ego's voice rang in my head. I gave the shirt one last good tug then asked, "Where are we going?"

"To celebrate."

"You got a job?" I squealed.

"Not just any job, I got the office assistant job at Sound Architects." Mom was beaming. She hadn't been this happy in forever. Flipping on her turn signal, we pulled onto the next street. "Quick, Neepa, help me find this place. The number is 404. It's an Italian bistro."

With our faces pressed against the windows, we drove down the road searching for the numbers on the buildings. On the left, there were several retail shops, and on the right, a tattoo parlor and a store called Nature's Green. *Oh, cool, a salad place*, I thought. *Nope, it's a cannabis store.*

"Mom, look, it's right there," I said, pointing at the last building on the street.

We pulled around back and parked in the lot. Mom grabbed my hand as soon as we got out of the car and almost skipped to the door. *Since she is never silly, this must be a good job.* The restaurant was small, but it felt like we were in Italy or what I thought Italy would be like. Josie and Enapay beat us and were already seated. I waved at Enapay, and his face changed from an "oh hey" look to a "wow" look when he saw me.

Josie commented, "Neepa, you look so pretty."

My face flushed, and I muttered, "Thank you." I was too embarrassed to look at Enapay.

"Okay, let's order. Dinner's on me," Mom announced.

Once we placed our orders, Josie jumped in. "So, tell us all about this job."

"Well," Mom paused for dramatic effect. "I was called today and told that I got the office assistant position at Sound Architects, a major architectural firm. My job entails managing phones, setting meetings, creating presentations, and other jobs as assigned. They said there's a lot of opportunity for growth, and after ninety days we get health insurance."

"Oh, Mina, that is wonderful. Congratulations," Josie gushed.

I looked over at Mom. "Well deserved," I added.

"Thank you, Neepa," Mom responded in an appreciative voice.

Dinner was fantastic, and we seemed to laugh the whole time. Enapay was cracking us up with his stories about his first time snowboarding. I could feel Mom watching me.

"What?"

"Can't I enjoy watching my daughter have a good time?" She smiled, and Josie gave her a thumbs-up. Walking back to the car, in the distance, I saw Michael from school walking toward us.

"Oh, no. It's him. Pretend you are not here, and he won't notice you," Ego suggested. I braced myself and did as Ego advised, with the hope he would not see or say anything to me.

Walking past, I could tell he didn't recognize me at first then he smiled and said, "Hey Chicago, you clean up good."

I didn't respond.

Mom looked at me. "A friend from school?"

"I wouldn't call him a friend."

"Huh."

The greenbelt had become my safe haven, a place where I could think and just be. My spot was on the hill next to an enormous pine tree. Its needles' blue silvery hue and size made it stand out next to all the other trees in the park. They had trimmed the branches just high enough to stand under, and the sweet piney smell made it even more inviting. I settled in and leaned against it.

The only separation between the townhouse properties and the park was a simple wrought-iron fence that had bent posts, providing a shortcut to the main street for those who dared to slip through. Normally there was not much activity, but that afternoon turned out to be different. There was a lot of commotion in the parking lot. Perched on the hill, I had a perfect view of the activities. Police cars, a moving truck, and a family were arguing with the police officers. That was an all-too-familiar scene, and I knew what it was like to be evicted. Anger, shame, fear all rolled up into an ugly, thorny knot in the stomach.

As the drama played out in front of me, my head filled with memories of us skipping out in the middle of the night because we couldn't pay rent or coming home and finding our stuff on the curb. I tried not to pay attention since it wasn't my business, but for some reason, I felt compelled to watch. There was a girl. Why did she look familiar? I tried to get closer without being noticed, then I realized who it was— Ann, one of T's *girls* and the one who knocked the books from my arms.

"Okay, you need to get out of here now. If she sees you, the target on your back will be huge." Ego's warning was accurate, so as soon as I recognized her, I bolted.

The next day, I got to history class early and took my seat. Ann walked in, stared, and then beelined right for me.

"Neepa, here she comes. Close your eyes and she won't see you," Ego instructed.

I didn't know what else to do, so I did it. I closed my eyes. "Hey, Quiet Girl." Through one slightly opened eye, I peered at her. "I saw you in the park the other day. If you mention what you saw to anybody, I'll kick your ass."

"I don't doubt you will, but why would I do that? I know how it feels, plus it's nobody's business but yours."

"Nice one," Ego complimented.

My response even surprised me. Ann didn't know how to react. Her prolonged look made it seem like she was trying to grasp what I had said. She turned and stormed away. Now that I didn't use my locker, T and her *girls* had to find other ways to torment me, which usually happened to and from class. On more than one occasion, T lunged at me, pretending that she was going to hit me, making me flinch or causing me to drop my stuff.

"Why so jumpy, Quiet Girl? What's wrong, can't you speak?"

Each time I gathered my stuff, I heard other students giggle or noticed them look at me with pity in their eyes. I didn't know which was worse. One of her *girls* was always filming, so I was sure there were more videos of me out there on social media. For the first time, I was happy I didn't have a phone—what I didn't know wouldn't hurt me. But there were days when either Enapay, Rebecca, or Julie would quickly put their phone away as I approached. They didn't say a thing, but I knew it was another video.

Visual arts class turned out to be a lot more interesting than I thought it would be. Mr. Taylor was an amazing artist and encouraged us to experiment and try new ways of expression. After school, I took the bus to the shops to try my hand at sketching whatever I saw. There was a small bench that allowed me to see the street's activity but not stand out. An older heavyset man with deep lines in his face was sitting on a bench across the street next to his bulldog. I laughed, thinking they could have been twins—my first models. A loud voice disrupted the initial stroke of my pencil. Michael and, what seemed like, his dad were getting into an expensive SUV. As they slowly drove past, I could hear his father's angry voice tearing into him. Luckily, Michael didn't see me, but his dejected face spoke volumes. My heart ached, and I could feel his pain. Experiencing that exchange stripped away all my desire to be creative, so I took a mental picture of the man and his dog to try later.

Since moving into the apartment, there had been a rabbit that regularly visited and sat next to the bush by the door. It must have had its hutch nearby because I didn't scare it when I came or went; it just sat there squinching its nose and looked at me. After watching it for many days, one afternoon it felt like it wanted to get my attention, so I kept its stare and asked, "Do you have a message for me?" There was a sensation deep within me that made me feel like it wanted to tell me something, but what?

When I got inside, I reached under the bed and retrieved the box Grandma had given me. Guilt crept in because the box was my secret. Grandma gave it to me, and I wanted to keep it private as long as I could. Looking through the poems, I was excited to see there was one about a rabbit.

Rabbit, rabbit, your fear is profound.

Making all your worries compound.

Focusing on what-ifs closes the soul.

Help me release my fears so they will not unfold.

Huh, I don't remember Grandpa ever telling me that one. Grabbing a granola bar from the cupboard, I fell into the kitchen chair. There on the table I noticed a note. "Neepa, your mom has a business dinner. She won't be home 'til later. You can come up and have dinner with us at six o'clock if you'd like. Josie."

"*Uh oh,*" Ego sighed.

My heart sank. Things were going so well. Maybe it really was a work dinner, but there was something that didn't feel right.

"*So who do you think it is this time? A new guy from work or someone else?*"

"Really, Ego, you are going there?" I said out loud.

"*Well, isn't that what you were thinking?*"

"No, remember things are different."

"*Uh-huh.*"

Dinner with Josie and Enapay was fantastic. I hadn't eaten such great-tasting food since Grandma made it. We actually had fresh vegetables. Even though they invited me to stay until Mom came home, I knew that would *not* be a good idea, so I used the homework excuse. At ten o'clock, I heard the door open. "Neepa, I'm home."

My face was covered in soap, head hung over the bathroom sink, so I quickly rinsed, grabbed my towel, and walked out of the bathroom. "Wow, that must have been some work dinner. Who were you with?"

"My boss wanted to reward me for doing such a great job, so we went out and had sushi."

"Mom, is he married?"

"Ouch, why would you ask that?"

"Because it's about that time."

"What do you mean, about that time?" Her demeanor turned from happy to defensive.

"It always happens when things are going well at your job. Somehow, you get yourself involved with a man from work, and they are generally married. Then you get fired, and we're heading back to Chicago again, but this time we have no place to go."

"Neepa, I'm your mother. You *will not* talk to me that way. I *am* an adult, and I know what I'm doing."

"Yeah, just like you knew what you were doing in Minnesota, Oregon, and Seattle. Mom, I like it here. Don't screw this up." I stormed back into the bathroom and slammed the door.

Mom stood next to the bathroom door and sweetly said, "Neepa, honey, don't be mad. I'm not going to screw this up. He's a nice man. Don't you want to have a father?"

"What?" I yelled, jerking the door open, coming face to face with her. "I don't need a father. I need a mother who doesn't sabotage our life when things finally get good. I need a home where I can live for more than two years. I need to not be bullied at every school I attend. Mom, I just need you. Why do you need a man so badly?"

"Neepa, I may be your mom, but I am *still* a woman, and I'd like to have a man in my life, plus I'm tired of bearing all this responsibility by myself."

"Well, maybe you should have thought about that before you got knocked up. Your choices are not my fault. Don't screw this up for me." I grabbed my jacket and stormed out of the house. As soon as I got outside, I bolted, desperately needing to get away as fast as I could. The further I got, the fainter my mom's voice became. The house lamps lit my way to the greenbelt and my tree. Luckily, it was a mild night. I curled up under the tree and cried myself to sleep.

"Butterfly, come walk with me."

"Oh, Grandpa," I said, sobbing. "She's doing it again."

"Neepa, calm down. Do not be mad at your mother. She's scared. Not having your grandmother or me to fall back on, she's afraid that she cannot do it on her own. She wants the best for you but feels she cannot give that to you. Your mother seeks someone who can provide so that you and she can be cared for."

"But Grandpa, she's strong. Why doesn't she think she can do it on her own?"

"She has always felt ashamed because she didn't finish school like others, getting a GED, having you when she was a teenager, not going to college. Treat her with love, Neepa. Just because she's an adult doesn't mean she can't be scared like a child. Do not worry; everything turns out like it should."

"What does that mean?" His image began to fade. "Grandpa?"

"Neepa, remember the rabbit."

A bright light hit my face, and something nudged my foot. Squinting, I could see two police officers.

"What's your name, young lady?"

"Neepa."

"Neepa what?"

"Neepa Irving."

"Alright. Your mother has been looking for you. Come on."

"Where are we going?" I replied, fear consuming me.

"We're taking you home."

Slowly, I got to my feet and brushed myself off. The officer opened the rear door of the patrol car, and I got in. A few minutes later, we pulled into our driveway, and I saw both Mom and Josie standing on the front porch.

"Now you're in for it," Ego declared.

"Ego, be quiet. I'm tired of being the victim of her poor decisions."

Mom came down to get me. After they let me out of the car, she thanked the officers for their help.

Both officers looked at me, and one said, "Neepa, take care of yourself."

As soon as they were out of sight, I wriggled out of Mom's grasp and went down to the apartment.

"Josie, thank you for your help. She has never done this before. To be honest, I'm worried about her. During our argument, she mentioned something about being bullied at school."

"I'll ask Enapay if he knows anything. Remember, Mina, she has been through a lot. Both of you have. Just take everything one day at a time. She needs security. Focus on that. If you want me to talk to her in my professional capacity as a therapist, I would be happy to do so. No charge," Josie added, smiling.

"Thank you, but I don't think she would be receptive to therapy right now.

"Understood. The offer stands if you change your mind."

When Mom returned to the apartment, I was already in bed with the covers over my head. No matter how hard Mom tried to get me to talk, I wouldn't say a word. She finally gave up and slept on the couch.

LARVA

The caterpillar eats to prepare for the next stage in life.

*The calories consumed will be used to
fuel an astonishing transformation.*

CHAPTER 5

Midway through class, I walked up to Mr. Taylor, and asked, "May I have a pass? I need to use the restroom."

"Yeah, sure. Here you go."

The visual arts room was in one of the furthest classrooms from anywhere. It was a hike to get to the bathroom. I went into the stall to do my business, and when I came out, T was leaning against the sink waiting for me.

"Well, if it isn't Quiet Girl? Funny I should find you in here, alone."

I washed my hands, and all I could hear was Ego saying, "*Stay calm, but get out as fast as you can.*"

When I tried to leave, T pushed me, making my head slam against the wall.

"Where do you think you're going?" she stated with hate in her eyes.

"Back to class."

"Not yet, you're not."

My eyes narrowed. "What do you want from me? What have I done to you?"

"I don't like the way you look."

"Okay, then don't look at me," I snapped back.

She didn't appreciate my humor and slugged me in the stomach. Buckled over, I dry heaved. She lifted my head by my hair and yelled, "Who do you think you are, coming in here all high and mighty? You're just weak!"

"What are you talking about?" I sputtered in between coughs. Wasting no time, T wound up to punch me in the face. Blocking most of the punch pissed her off even more. As she squared up to hit me again, the door opened. It was Rachel from the admissions office. She gasped then yelled, "What the hell is going on here?"

T turned and pushed past Rachel then ran out of the bathroom.

"Oh, my god, Neepa, are you okay?"

"I've had worse," I groaned. Rachel helped me over to the sink to wash my face.

"Has Tamara been bothering you?"

"You could say that," I responded in a half chuckle, half cough.

"Why didn't you tell anyone?" she asked.

"Because it makes it worse. Plus, we're new here. My mom is busy with her new job and . . ."

"Neepa, you can't continue to live in fear of Tamara. You need to file a report on her. We have a zero-tolerance bullying policy."

"Oh yeah, zero tolerance. That's what they all said."

"If you don't file an incident report, I will."

"Neepa, red alert!" Ego screamed.

"Do what you will, but I'm not doing it."

By the time I got back to visual arts, the class was over, and I was already late for history. Rachel had given me a late pass so I would not get detention from Ms. Jones. When I knocked on the door, Ms. Jones's jaw dropped. My eye must have started to swell. She tried to play it off. "Miss Irving, nice of you to join us." I handed her the pass and walked back to my seat. Ann looked away as I passed.

At home, I tried everything to get my eye to stop swelling, but it was no use. Mom would find out and then everything would blow up. In my haste to hide my injury, I had missed the note on the table. *Good, she won't be home for a while.* For the first time, I was happy that she was out with *whomever*. I needed time and lots of it.

It was after eleven o'clock when she slipped into bed. In the morning, I got up early to see how bad my eye looked. It was already turning black and blue, but at least the swelling went down. Quietly, I searched through Mom's makeup bag to find some concealer and did my best to hide my black eye. Normally, I don't wear hoodies, but I found an old one and pulled the hood up to hide my face. When Mom woke, she tried to give me a hug. I pulled away and pretended to be mad at her for coming home so late, all the while not letting her see my face.

"Neepa, honey. Don't be mad. We had a late meeting preparing for a big presentation that my boss has today. Then we grabbed a bite to eat."

A funny feeling came over me, and I could tell Mom wasn't telling me the whole story. I could feel her shame. Under different circumstances, I would have pushed harder, but I had bigger issues to deal with. Miraculously, I slipped out of the house without her noticing my eye, but when Enapay saw me, he was like, "Damn, girl, that looks bad. Did you try to cover it up?"

"I tried, but I don't know how to use makeup."

"You can't go to school like that. Come on. Let's see if my mom can do something." We rushed back into his house, and he yelled, "Mom, we need you."

Josie came running down the stairs. "What's wrong?" As soon as she saw me, she gasped for air. "Neepa, what happened?"

"I got beat up at school."

"When did this happen?"

"Yesterday."

"Yesterday? What did your mom say?" she asked.

"She doesn't know."

"What do you mean, she doesn't know? Hasn't she looked at you today?"

"She was out 'til late last night, and I hid my face from her this morning."

"Oh, Neepa. You must tell her."

"I can't. She already has so much on her plate."

"Please, Mom, can't you just put some makeup on her, and we can figure it out later?"

Josie looked at both of us and then went to get her make-up bag. To make me look presentable, it took longer than the time we had to get to the bus, so Josie had to drive us to school. We made it just in time for the first bell.

"You good?" Josie asked before we got out of the car.

"Yup. Thanks."

"Neepa, we'll talk about this when you both get home from school." Enapay and I looked at each other, knowing this would not just blow over.

As usual, word traveled fast, and people kept their distance. Not like anyone talked to me other than Enapay, Rebecca, and Julie. As we walked into school, I could see Mr. Fern and Rachel waiting for me. "Oh great," I said under my breath.

"What's going on?" Enapay asked.

"Rachel walked in on T kicking my butt. She said that she'd file a report if I didn't."

"Well, aren't you going to file one?"

"No way, that only makes things worse."

"Worse than what it already is? Neepa, you got to stand up for yourself."

"People always say that when they aren't the ones getting beat up," I replied as I walked off.

"Good morning, Neepa. Can we talk to you?" Mr. Fern asked.

"Do I have a choice?"

"Not really. Come on, let's go to my office." Rachel walked behind me as I followed him to his office.

"Neepa, I have been informed that there was a physical altercation yesterday between you and Tamara. Is that correct?"

"Don't say a word, T will know, and she will kick your butt again," Ego warned.

I didn't respond.

"We know Tamara has been bothering you. The videos of her slamming you into the lockers and other intimidating actions she's taken toward you are already on file. You can lodge a complaint against her, or Rachel can since she was witness to the altercation. It is up to you. What does your mother want you to do?"

"Shit, he is bringing Mom into this. You have to do something, quick," Ego advised.

In a low voice, I replied, "She's aware and wants me to let it go."

"Are you sure?" Rachel challenged. "That is not what we would recommend."

"Since we're new in town, and she just got a job, she doesn't want us to cause any trouble," I explained.

They looked at each other, trying to determine if they should believe me or not. I looked at each of them directly in the eyes and then asked, "May I go now? I'm late for English."

Mr. Fern paused and then asked Rachel to get me a late pass. Before I left, Mr. Fern looked at me and said, "Neepa, it won't stop just because you don't say anything."

I kept my head down and walked out.

Whispers filled the day. People covering their mouths like I might be able to read lips as they talked about me. Or like I had a disease. Everyone looked. No one spoke, but as soon as I walked past, the whispers started again. This day needed to be over. Walking into visual arts class, my body relaxed, and I could breathe. The kids in this class didn't care about the dramas of high school. They were too busy creating. My head was down deep in concentration when I felt a light tap on my shoulder. Looking up, there was a girl standing next to me I hadn't seen before. She was pretty but looked shy and frail.

"Neepa?"

"Yes."

"My name is Leah, and I'm sorry to hear what you're going through with T."

I stopped what I was doing, stared her in the face, and spoke harshly. "It's nothing I can't handle. Now please mind your own business."

She gave me a weird look like *are you crazy*, but I ignored it. She then turned and walked back to her seat.

"Nice job shithead, no wonder you're so good at making friends," Ego remarked.

"Shut up. I've had a tough day," I blurted out, realizing that I didn't use my inside voice. A few people looked, but they just went back to their work.

When Enapay and I got off the bus, Josie was waiting for us on the porch. Without a word, we followed her into the house.

"Sit down, you two. Now, what is going on?" Josie demanded.

Enapay turned to me with a "well, tell her" look.

After a couple of deep breaths, I spilled it, telling her how it all started the first day of school when a group of girls gave me the stink eye, which progressed to being pushed into the lockers by the leader of the group, and finally when T beat me up in the bathroom.

"Enapay, did you know all of this?" I glared at him, not to say a word.

"All I knew was the gossip going around and the videos."

"Videos?" Josie yelled. "Neepa, I know I'm not your mother, and you don't have to do anything that I say, but if you want me to keep my mouth shut and help you, you better start explaining."

I nodded my head in agreement.

Josie took a deep breath. "Now, let's start from the beginning. Why did they give you the stink eye?"

"I have no idea; I didn't do anything but walk past them," I explained.

"Mom, this group of girls is known for bullying. It seems like they find one person and then pick on them the entire year."

"It continues to surprise me that schools don't find a way to stop this type of behavior," she stated.

"They can't do anything if the kid doesn't complain."

"Has it escalated to violence before?"

Enapay lowered his head. "No, not that I know of."

"Okay, Neepa. Tell me what happened in the bathroom."

I let out a big sigh and told the whole story again. It probably wouldn't be the last time I'd tell it.

"So, school personnel saw what happened?"

"Yes," I admitted.

"And did they do anything?"

"They asked if I wanted to file a report. I said no."

"You said what?"

"I told them I didn't want to file a report."

"Did they call your mother?"

"No, I told them Mom knew and that we agreed not to file a report."

"Neepa, why would you do that?"

"Look, Josie, I know you're trying to help me, but I've been bullied at every school I have ever attended. In the beginning, we would complain, but they would find other ways to hurt or mess with me. So, I just stopped telling Mom because nothing was ever done, and then we usually move, and I didn't have to deal with those kids anymore."

After a few deep breaths, Josie calmed down. "Okay, okay. I hear you, but you can't live your life like this, especially now that it has become physical. Enapay, who is this girl?"

"Her name is Tamara, but everyone calls her T."

"Even though this goes against my better judgment, I *will not* tell your mother. Just promise me you'll not be in the halls alone, and if she starts up with you again, you better tell me. I don't care how harmless you think it may be, you tell me. Promise?" Josie stared at me.

"Yes."

"Yes, what?"

"Yes, I promise."

"Enapay?"

"I promise."

Josie went into her bag, took out the concealer she used on me that morning, and gave it to me. "Here, take this. You will need it for a few more days."

"Thank you," I replied.

When I got back to the apartment, I went to the bathroom to check my eye. It looked better, but if Mom really looked at me, she would know something was up. I kept the hood of my sweatshirt up even in the house and decided that I would continue to act mad at her for being out so late, which I actually was, but I couldn't get into that under the circumstances.

At school, the chatter about me slowed down for the time being; it seemed they found someone else to gossip about. I kept my promise to Josie and was never alone. I also heard that T was not in school because she was supposedly sick, but everyone knew she was suspended.

CHAPTER 6

Once Mom had started working, she got me a cell phone. Nothing special, but at least I was connected to the world and able to call Grandma more often. School was flying by, and I was so excited to tell Grandma how I was doing. She had always encouraged me to apply myself in school and for me to make honor roll. I knew she would be proud to know I was on track. When I called to tell her the news, it seemed like it took longer than usual for her to answer the phone, and when she did, her voice sounded dry and hoarse.

"Hello?"

"Hi, Grandma, it's Neepa."

"Oh, Neepa, it is so good to hear your voice. How are you doing?"

"I am well. How are you?"

"Couldn't be better," Grandma replied, but I felt she was hiding something.

"I called to tell you I'm on track to make honor roll!"

"Honor roll? Neepa, that is wonderful. I'm so proud of you. See, the butterfly is growing. I can't wait for you to stretch those wings." There was a pause then I heard labored breathing. "I haven't spoken to your mother in a while. How is she?"

"She is good. Mom is doing so well at her job—she already received a promotion."

"Very good." Grandma stopped to breathe again. "Are you happy, Neepa?"

I hesitated, then said, "Yes, Grandma, I am happy."

"Well done. I'm so proud of you both. I love you, Neepa."

Hearing how tired Grandma sounded, I responded, "I love you too, Grandma. I miss you and will call again soon, okay?"

"Okay. Neepa?"

"Yes, Grandma."

"Remember to stretch those wings and fly. Grandpa and I will see you soon."

A week later, when Mom came home from work, her eyes were puffy and bloodshot.

"Mom, what's wrong? Something happen at work?"

"No, Neepa. I got a phone message from Grandma's neighbor, Ms. Brown. Grandma is with Grandpa now. She passed last night in her sleep."

My knees buckled, and I fell to the floor. Mom gently picked me up, took me to the couch, and hugged me. We cried in each other's arms. Looking at Mom with my tear-stained face, I choked out, "I knew it," before crying again.

"Neepa, what do you mean?"

"The last time we talked, she asked if I was happy. I said yes, and she said she was proud of us. Before she hung up, she said that she and Grandpa would see me soon. If we were with her . . ." I trailed off, uncontrollably sobbing. Mom stroked my hair and lifted my face.

"Shh, shh, Neepa. Calm down. Breathe. Sweetheart, there was nothing you or I could do. When I spoke with her last, she said she missed Grandpa desperately, and when she knew we were going to be okay, it was her time to be with him. Grandma gave us the tough love we needed to get back on our feet and stand tall. She knew what she was doing."

"But Mom, I miss her." My breathing became labored, and it felt like my chest was collapsing. I buried my head in my hands.

"Neepa, she and Grandpa were so proud of you and knew you would do amazing things. Prove them right, be strong, and know they're always with you."

The next day, we took the long drive back to Chicago. We needed to take care of the house and hold the service. Mom was already in contact with the Indian Center to reserve space for the funeral. We would cremate Grandma just like Grandpa and then take them both back to Massachusetts to lay them to rest on tribal lands. It was almost ten o'clock at night when we arrived. Ms. Brown met us at the house to let us in.

"Mina, Neepa, you both look so good. I guess Denver was a good move for you."

"Thank you, Ms. Brown. Yes, Denver has been treating us well. Thank you for taking care of Ma when I couldn't."

"Your parents always treated me well and did so much for this community. I was happy to help in her last hours. Will you two be moving back, or will you stay in Denver?"

Mom and I looked at each other. "Too early to tell, Ms. Brown. Neepa and I haven't even discussed it."

"Okay, well, call if you need anything. Here are the keys."

As she turned to go, Mom asked, "Ms. Brown, I know you've already done a lot, but could you help us one more time with the service at the Indian Center? I want to make sure the word gets out. I know there will be many people who want to attend."

"Of course. Happy to help."

"Thank you."

Walking into the house felt uncomfortable, and it smelled stale. Mom sent me to our old room to get some sleep, as we had a lot to do the next day. On my way, I passed Grandma and Grandpa's room. It was dark and felt cold. I couldn't look, so I hurried down the hall. Slipping into our familiar bed lulled me to sleep within minutes.

When I woke, it took a moment for my eyes to adjust. Not immediately recognizing where I was, the sounds coming from the kitchen made my heart leap, and I jumped out of bed with the excitement of seeing Grandma. Then I remembered and was yanked back to the horrible reality that she was gone. Mom was already dressed and working on her second cup of coffee.

"Morning, Neepa. There is cereal in the cupboard, but check the date on the milk before you pour."

The milk was past its date, so I settled for some toast with peanut butter.

"Honey, we have a lot to do today. If you are okay, can you stay here and clean out the kitchen of all the perishable stuff? Box up the dry goods, and we can decide if we will take them or if we want to donate everything. When we leave in a few days, I want to make sure that the house will be fine until we can come back again."

"Okay, where are you going?"

"I'll be with Ms. Brown getting everything ready for Grandma's service."

I knew not to argue and to just do as I was told. Things had to get done, so Mom was hyper focused. Once she left, the house felt foreign as I saw things I had not seen before. Grandma had always kept a tidy house, and there wasn't a lot of extra fluff or tchotchkes around. The more I looked, the more I realized there were few pictures either. To keep my sadness at bay, I stayed in the kitchen doing as Mom asked.

Grandma had a small transistor radio she kept on the counter to keep her company. I turned it on to lighten my mood and opened the window over the sink to get some fresh air. Being just one person in the house, Grandma didn't have much food in the refrigerator or freezer. The cupboards, however, were stocked with commodity food from the elder program at the Indian Center—containers of peanut butter, pasta, tuna fish, apple juice, vegetables, and beans. I pulled out everything, put them on the table, checked the dates, and organized what was left. Mom was gone for a while, so after I finished cleaning out the kitchen, I climbed the stairs to

Grandma and Grandpa's room. The sun put a warm hue in the room, making it less unsettling. Seeing the bed, I realized that this was where she passed. She was lying on the right side, because Grandpa slept on the left, and here was where she died.

Forcing down the lump in my throat, I carefully walked around their room. Everything had its place. A small hand mirror, brush, and comb were placed on her dresser. Her gray hair weaved throughout the bristles of the brush. A framed picture of Grandma and Grandpa on their wedding day was on full display. To my surprise, when I looked into the large mirror that hung over the dresser, there was a picture of Grandpa and me when I was a little girl slipped into the frame. He was holding my hand as we walked in the park. Gently, I took it from the mirror and put it in my pocket.

"Neepa, honey, I'm back. Where are you?"

"Upstairs," I yelled.

"Well, come on down. I need you to help me with something."

When I got down to the bottom of the stairs, I saw Mom putting a container on the mantel.

"What is that?"

"It's Grandma's ashes. I just came from the funeral home."

Neither one of my grandparents subscribed to organized religion like Christianity or Catholicism. They believed in nature, the Great Spirit, and knew that all their questions would be answered if they just listened. Cremation and having their ashes spread across their homeland was their final request. A shiver went down my spine. Mom could tell I was a little freaked out. When Grandpa died, I was younger with no responsibilities. All I did was attend the funeral. I didn't even know where Grandpa's ashes were kept.

"Neepa, remember Grandma's ashes are just a physical representation. Her soul is within you, and just like Grandpa, she's always with you."

I nodded. Then, after a few moments, I asked, "Mom, if they're within me, are they also within you?"

"Yes, honey, they are."

Mom was on the phone all afternoon and into the early evening, getting things ready for the funeral. Ms. Brown stopped by and brought us dinner: sausage and kale soup.

"Won't you join us for dinner?" Mom asked.

"Thanks, but I must get back to my family, plus the next few days are going to be busy. Are you all set?"

"Yes, I believe we are. Thank you again. We couldn't have done it without your support."

"No worries. Happy to help. I expect there'll be a large turnout. Will people be coming back to the house?"

"No, I have arranged for the repast to also be held at the Indian Center."

Okay, well then, we will see you soon."

I could hardly wait for Ms. Brown to leave. The soup smelled amazing, and I was starving. We didn't have time for lunch, so a solid meal would do us both good.

"Neepa, set the table, and I'll be right in; I just need to make this last phone call."

The smell of the soup and the activity within the house made it seem less dark and cold. It was almost like it used to be when Grandma was alive. I dished out two bowls and waited for Mom to join me. She poked her head into the kitchen and gestured for me to start without her. That was not a problem. Mm, this was almost as good as Grandma's—almost. I already had two bowls in me before Mom finally came to eat.

"Is everything okay?" I asked.

Mom looked up from her phone. "It will be. There's a lot of house stuff and arrangements I'm still working on. So, what do you think? Should we move back to Chicago? This is our house now."

"Is there anything left for us here?" I asked, hoping that Mom would say no.

"We can make something. This house is ours, free and clear."

"But what about your new job? Would you be able to find something as good here?"

"That's a good question." She paused, thinking about what I had just said. "In time, but I feel you really like Denver. Correct?"

"Yes, I do. For the first time, I feel like I'm making real friends."

"Is everything going well at school?"

"Nothing that I can't handle," I answered, not wanting to alarm Mom.

"Neepa," Mom said in an accusing voice.

"Mom, I'm good."

"Well, we don't have to decide now."

"Could we sell this house and buy something in Denver?" I asked in my sweetest voice.

"Maybe, Neepa, maybe."

The next day entailed more of the same, me cleaning the house and Mom on the phone preparing for Grandma's funeral the following day. In the room where I'd grown up, there was a stack of boxes in the closet. I had never noticed them before. Filled with Grandpa's mementos, it didn't feel right to poke around without Mom, but they seemed important, so I put them in the stack of what we would keep.

Mom calling my name roused me from my deep sleep. "Neepa, come on, we gotta get going."

"Okay," I responded in a raspy voice. Slowly, I rolled out of bed and jumped into the shower. There were going to be many people we knew at the funeral, so I needed to look presentable. Mom gave me a simple black dress to wear with a pair of black slip-on dress shoes. It was easy for her to buy my clothes now since we both wore the same size. I braided my hair and wore a simple wampum necklace that Grandma and

Grandpa gave me for my twelfth birthday. When I came down the stairs, Mom looked like she hadn't even gone to bed. She was still in the same clothes.

"Oh, Neepa, you look so grown up. Absolutely beautiful."

"Mom, did you even go to sleep?"

"I got a couple of hours on the couch. Let me run upstairs and change, and then we gotta head over."

When I walked into the living room, there was a large, framed picture of Grandma and a bunch of smaller framed photos of her and Grandpa. I felt my chest constrict, trying to hold back my tears. It was no use. The floodgates opened, and I quietly sobbed. Mom came down the stairs, also dressed in a modest black dress. She wore her hair in a bun and a simple pair of beaded earrings. Watching her walk down the stairs, she looked older; her face was drawn and her eyes dulled. She saw me looking at her and could tell I had been crying.

"Neepa, come here, honey." Mom wrapped me in a loving hug and whispered in my ear, "Remember, they're always with us."

We loaded the car with the photos of Grandma and Grandpa and Grandma's urn and headed over to the center. By the time we arrived, people were already congregating. Ms. Brown met us inside and helped Mom arrange the photos.

"Mina, it is going to be a large turnout. So many people were touched by your mother."

Ms. Brown looked over at me and could see fear in my eyes. "Neepa," she said as she took my hand in hers. "Your grandmother was family to so many who had lost their way.

People who couldn't go home to their reservations but didn't fit in the city either. She provided comfort, wisdom, and a shoulder to cry on. People will want to tell you how she helped them. Listen and know that they see the same qualities in you as well."

When the drum arrived, it was time to begin the service. There were more people than seats, so they lined the walls and filled the reception area. The drum began, and everyone who wasn't already standing stood. It was a beautiful northern honor song. I was already emotional, but the vibration of the drum and strength of the singers' voices in honor of Grandma made me sob like a baby. Mom pulled me close, trying to comfort me.

Several people gave readings or told stories of Grandma. Ms. Brown stood. "Helen Irving was the first person my husband and I met when we arrived in Chicago. I can see her now, walking with purpose toward us, giving my husband, who was my boyfriend at the time, a scare. Once she reached us, she gave both of us big hugs and welcomed us to the community. Our relationship grew from there, and I had the honor of taking care of her in her last moments on this earth. She was our family away from family, and I'll miss her greatly."

Then Mom got up to say a few words. As she stood at the podium, her eyes filled with tears. She paused, gaining her composure, then began.

"Many of you know that Ma and I had a difficult relationship. She was a powerful woman who expected your best. She did not expect the best compared to others; it was the best that you could give at that moment. For many reasons, I was unable to give my best, and we argued all the time. It was only after she kicked us out and gave me the tough love I needed that I realized what she was doing. By the turnout in this room, she gave that same love to many, and we have all become better for it. My mother was tough but fair, and under that hard exterior was a beautiful heart that held a never-ending amount of love. When I miss her, I look at my daughter, Neepa, who is just like her, and I'm reminded that I need to strive to do my best for me and her. Thank you, Ma. I love you."

The rest of the funeral and repast were a blur. So many people, everyone wanting to give their condolences. Mom was managing much better than I was. An older woman slowly approached. She took my hand and placed a small carving inside it, then closed my hand within hers, and said, "Your grandmother wanted you to have this. It will give you the strength to accept your power."

"I'm sorry, my what?"

She didn't respond and quietly walked away. I opened my hand to see the carving of a bear. It was made of black stone, smooth and shiny, with turquoise eyes. Knowing that Grandma gave this to me offered me comfort, but my mind swirled, trying to understand what the elder meant when she said power.

We stayed a few more days, cleaning and sorting, and then headed back to Colorado. The time back in Chicago was a whirlwind. So many people connected to Grandma and Grandpa. What I realized was they were my only connection to Chicago. Now that both were gone, I didn't need to come back. We packed the most important things and closed the house. When Mom locked the door, it felt like she was closing a chapter in her life. Ms. Brown would look after the place until we decided what we would do with the house.

Driving back to Denver was long and quiet. Neither Mom nor I needed to say anything. When we arrived, we both gave a sigh of relief. Without saying it, this was our new home, and it felt good to be back.

We took an extra day before returning to work and school. In the morning, Mom went up to spend some time with Josie to discuss house stuff and catch up, which gave me time to be by myself and quiet my mind. Since receiving the bear carving, it had been in my pocket close to me. Once Mom left, I pulled out the shoebox and searched for a poem about a bear.

Bear, bear, your strength is profound.

Taking solitude deep in the ground.

Your introspection allows you to quiet the mind.

Share your power of knowing and help me find answers inside.

No wonder I felt better holding the bear carving. It symbolizes strength, introspection, and the power of knowing. Is that what the elder meant when she said power, the power of knowing? What does that mean?

CHAPTER 7

Back at school, I was quieter than usual and kept my distance from Enapay, Rebecca, and Julie to further put my head into my studies. Mom seemed to be equally as quiet. She came home every night—no more late work dinners, at least for the time being. And we were okay with being quiet; it was just nice to be together. More than a month had passed, and slowly, life was getting back to what it once was. Luckily for me, T left me alone. Knowing that she had dodged a bullet by not being expelled, she kept a low profile.

All my classes were going well, and Mom was doing great at work, so she wanted to celebrate our joint success by going out to dinner.

"Neepa, let's try this little hole in the wall around the corner that I heard has great empanadas. It's nothing fancy so no need to change your clothes."

Mom wasn't kidding when she said it was a hole in the wall. As soon as you walked in the door, there were four small tables, a counter, and a cooler on the side that held bottled soft drinks. I ordered my favorite kind of empanada—ground beef with onion, peppers, boiled egg, and raisins. Mom ordered a pork-and-apple empanada to start. Everything smelled so good. I had a feeling we would go back for more. Our first two went down quickly, and I returned to the counter to order another round. In the back, I noticed a man yelling at a young woman who was wearing an apron. She was crying. As she turned to leave, our eyes locked. It was T. Her eyes narrowed, and I knew I was in trouble. When our order was ready, I told Mom I wasn't feeling well, so we took them to go.

The next day at school, I was on edge. Enapay could tell something was wrong, but he didn't dare push to get it out of me. Since T had been lying low, I had started using my locker again. But it was too good to be true. Julie and I went to my locker before our last class of the day. When I swung open the door, a piece of paper fell to the floor. Julie picked it up and handed it to me. "What is this?" I asked. She shrugged. I unfolded it and read, "YOUR DEAD."

"*Shit, shit, shit*" Ego screamed in my head.

Julie looked at me and noticed the color drain from my face. "Neepa, what's wrong? What does it say?"

My head swiveled from side to side, trying to assess who else was around. Immediately, I grabbed everything from my locker, stuffed it in my backpack, and rushed away, making Julie run to keep up. Once we were almost to class, Julie grabbed my arm to slow me down and asked again. "Seriously, Neepa, what is going on?"

"It's nothing."

"Nothing? Are you kidding me? Your face turned white, which is practically impossible since your skin is brown, and you ran away from your locker. What did the paper say?"

"It said, 'you're dead,'" I replied.

"What? Holy crap. What are you going to do?"

"Nothing."

"Nothing? She just threatened you. You need to tell someone."

"Tell them what? That someone wrote a note and put it in my locker. We don't even know who did it."

"You know exactly who did it or you wouldn't have reacted that way."

"Well, I don't have proof. No one can do anything until there is proof that T did it."

"Jeez, Neepa, this is crazy. Please be careful."

I gave a weak smile and walked into class.

To tell or not tell Josie was my dilemma. I had promised, but if I kept it quiet until I had more proof, we could actually do something. Enapay would find out because Julie would tell him and Rebecca. The real question was whether he would keep his mouth shut. On the bus ride home, I asked Enapay if he could come down and help me with some homework. He agreed, but he knew full well that there was more to this than homework.

Enapay opened the door and blurted out, "So, what are you going to do?"

"Well, it depends on what you're going to do. Are you going to tell your mom?"

"Neepa, I don't know what to do. Seriously, I don't want you to get hurt, and I don't want my mother to kill me."

"Just give me some time to get the proof I need then I'll tell Josie. I promise."

"And what if you don't get the proof?"

"Don't worry, I will."

"I hope so, for your sake."

Ever since the day T beat me up, Ann had kept her distance from me and hadn't really been hanging out with T as much. I took that as a sign that she didn't like what T did, and I wanted to test that theory. My plan was to get to history class early and speak to Ann before Ms. Jones arrived. Unfortunately, Ann was late. It was an enormous risk, but I passed her a note, asking that she meet with me the next day during lunch.

"Are you high?" Ego screamed. *"This is definitely not a good plan."*

I knew this might not go well. She could tell T about my request to meet, or she could meet me and then tell T everything we discussed, or worse, she could set me up so that T would have another opportunity to kick my ass. Unfortunately, I didn't see another option, so I took the chance.

The next day at our usual lunch table, I saw Ann over by the door. She acknowledged me and head gestured for me to come out to the hall. Just as I was getting up from the table, Julie and Rebecca showed up.

"Hey, where are you going?" Julie asked.

"Oh, I have to use the restroom. I'll be right back."

"Do you want one of us to go with you?" Rebecca asked.

"No, no, I'm good, but thanks."

Once Ann saw me getting up from the table, she walked out into the hall, giving enough distance between us to hide the fact that we were meeting. She waited a few feet from the cafeteria door then as soon as I walked out, she looked at me and indicated I should follow.

"Don't do it," Ego warned. *"This could be a trap."*

For some reason, I was not concerned. It felt like she wanted to talk to me as well. When I finally caught up with her halfway down an adjacent hall, we both knew we didn't have much time before the hall monitor or someone else saw us.

"So, what do you want?" Ann barked. "I shouldn't even be talking to you."

"I know, I know, but I just need to know why T hates me."

Ann scoffed. "She doesn't hate you. She doesn't even care about you. You are weak, and she takes advantage of the weak."

"Okay, so what if she thinks I'm weak? There are plenty of people who are weak. So you're telling me she has now threatened to kill me just because she thinks I'm weak?"

"What do you mean, threaten to kill you?"

"You don't know about the note in my locker?"

"Look, I've been keeping my distance from her. She's in a bad place. How do you know it was her?"

"I don't, but it's a pretty good assumption since she already beat me up once."

Fear flashed across Ann's face. "Look, I gotta go. Just watch your back."

When I returned to the cafeteria, it was like nothing happened. Enapay, Julie, and Rebecca were eating lunch, complaining about a test, and I slipped in without anyone asking questions. However, Ann's reaction to my question and the note made me really nervous.

That evening, before I went to sleep, I asked Grandpa to come to me and guide me.

"Hello, my butterfly."

"Grandpa, I wish you were here with me."

"But I am."

"No, I mean in the flesh. I need a hug."

"Oh, what is wrong?"

"T is bullying me because she thinks I'm weak."

"Neepa, people bully because deep down *they* are scared, and to hide the fear, they want to have power over someone else."

"But Grandpa, am I weak?"

"You tell me. Are you weak?"

"No."

"Well, then you have your answer. Neepa, you are special, and it's not because you are my granddaughter. You allow yourself to feel more than most people. You feel others' energy. You have intuition and you see. Think of all of this as your superpower, like a spidey sense. That does not make you weak, that makes you strong. You have the strength to feel what is inside versus pushing the pain away or taking it out on others. Do not worry, Neepa, you *are* powerful. Sleep soundly, my butterfly."

When I woke, I felt secure and comforted, just like I used to feel when Grandpa gave me a hug.

CHAPTER 8

I had promised Josie never to be alone at school, but I had to finish my visual arts project, plus there was a football game going on, so there were plenty of people around. The visual arts room was away from the main part of the school, making the roars of the game muted. By the time I finished, the game was over, and the school was strangely quiet. The dimmed lights made the hall look eerie. All I wanted to do was to get out of there and get home. Heading for the exit next to the gym, I felt immediately agitated, and the hairs on my neck stood on end. As I got closer to the locker room entrance, I could hear a disturbance inside. The crash of something being thrown against the wall then the distinct sound of sobbing.

"Turn around and use the other exit," Ego shrieked.

I briefly thought about it, but that exit would put me in the totally opposite direction of where I needed to go. Dismissing Ego's warnings, I took a deep breath and continued. Tension filled my body as I passed. My spidey senses were going crazy. I could feel pain, fear, and sadness. Then the hairs on my arms stood on end. Against my better judgment, I went back and entered the boy's locker room. It felt strange. The moisture from the showers lingered, and the smell of a hard-played game mixed with soap fragrance remained. I crept through quietly, trying to locate the crying. In the far corner, a bench was knocked over and a dark figure was crouched down against the lockers.

"Are we really doing this?" Ego asked. *"This is crazy."*

When I got closer, I realized it was Michael. His hair was still wet from the shower. He was barefoot, sitting with only his sweatpants on. Crying, he held a knife in his hand—a hunting knife, a big, jagged blade—twirling it between his fingers. He didn't seem to notice me until I was just a few feet away. Suddenly he looked up, realized it was me, and yelled.

"Chicago, what the hell are you doing in here? Stay away from me."

"Michael, I felt something was wrong. Are you okay?"

"I want you to go. Get out of here," he lashed out.

My face perplexed, I asked, "Why would I do that? A friend needs my help, so shouldn't I do everything to help them?"

"Friend? Who says we're friends?"

"You may not consider me a friend, but I think of you as one."

"Why?" he spat back at me.

"Just because I'm quiet doesn't mean I'm not observant. You were the first person outside of Enapay to actually see me. At times, you were even nice. You put on a loud and outgoing exterior, but I believe you are searching just like me. Trying to be accepted and not so lonely."

"What are you, a psychiatrist?"

"No, but I saw how your father treated you." His eyes widened. "I could feel your pain. No one wants to be demeaned like that; it hurts and it's confusing. The person who is supposed to love and support you shouldn't make you feel like that."

"You don't know what you're talking about. My father works hard. He travels a lot, and he expects things to be a certain way."

"And when they're not, he takes it out on you."

Michael hung his head, knowing what I said was right. His body deflated as if he wanted to melt into the locker room floor. He mumbled.

"Chicago, I'm tired. Trying to meet his expectations. Never proud of me. Straight A's, varsity football. Never enough. Always complains. He says I'm just like my mother. She left him. I didn't. He's never attended a game. Not one!" Tears spilled from his eyes. "What did I do wrong? Why can't he love me?" Tears, tears, and more tears came. He couldn't hold them back. They flowed freely. His confession wasn't for me but for himself. His gaze distant, he whispered, "It would just be easier if I were dead."

I listened, and then noticed the scars on his left wrist. This wasn't his first attempt. Contemplating what to say, I uttered, "I feel lonely a lot as well. Every school I've attended, I've been bullied. For no other reason than they wanted to have power over me. I didn't do anything. They didn't even get to know me to see what type of person I am. There were times when I thought about disappearing, taking my life because it had to be easier than this, right?" Michael just listened. "It could be easier. My grandma and grandpa say they're very happy and are at peace now that they're dead." My words snatched Michael out of his daze. He looked at me like I was a lunatic.

"What? You talk to your dead grandparents?"

"Yes, often. My grandfather especially helps to guide me through life." Michael just stared. "Hey, I don't want you to kill yourself, and I'm sure there are plenty of other people who don't want that to happen as well, including your father. Unfortunately, he has his own issues that he hasn't worked through, and he is taking them out on you. It's *not* your fault. You *are* a gifted person, someone who has a lot to offer this world. Your father probably doesn't know how to show his love. But just because he has issues to deal with doesn't mean that you have to die. I'm saying this to you, but I need to hear myself say it as well. It's time that you love yourself. You don't need anyone else's acceptance to prove that you're worthy of living this life."

We sat in silence for a long time, both staring off into the distance. The clank of a garbage can being emptied made us both jump, and I knew the janitor would come in to clean the locker room soon. I looked at Michael. "Come on, we gotta go." He slowly looked around like he was in a fog and then realized someone was coming. He grabbed his sweatshirt and running shoes.

"What do I do with this knife?" he asked, his voice filled with fear.

"Don't worry about that yet. Just move."

Michael and I ran out of the school through a back door. In the parking lot, he clumsily dressed. His face was so child-like and innocent. He looked at me with a strange wonderment in his eyes. I found myself staring at him, noticing his strong features and warm eyes.

"What are you doing?" Ego yelled. *"Stop looking at him. You know the plan. No boys until after you graduate from high school."*

I shook my head to quiet Ego but to also snap myself out of it.

"Wipe the knife off and throw it down a drain on your way home," I instructed. He didn't respond. "Did you hear me? Wipe the knife and drop it down a drain." His stare went right through me. "Are you good? Michael, are you good?" I asked in a louder voice.

His face transformed back to the Michael I knew. "Yeah, yeah. I'm good." We headed in different directions. I watched him as he walked away, hoping that he would be alright.

The next day, as soon as I got off the bus, I ran to my first period class, leaving Enapay wondering what was up. Each time the classroom door opened, my heart jumped. As the minutes passed and the class filled, Michael still hadn't shown up. I got a knot in the pit of my stomach. *Maybe he didn't go home. Maybe he didn't dispose of the knife. I shouldn't have left him alone.*

Horrible thoughts raced through my head, and Ego was there, fueling the fire. *"You shouldn't have left him. They may blame you if something happened to him."*

For the rest of the morning, I could barely concentrate. When I walked into lunch, Rebecca and Julie looked at me with concerned faces.

"Neepa, are you okay?" Rebecca asked.

I shook my head but didn't say a word. When Enapay joined us, I didn't even greet him. He looked at the other two, and they both shrugged their shoulders. Right before lunch period ended, as I was getting up, I felt someone pass by, and in a quiet voice, I heard, "Thanks, Chicago." My heart leapt, knowing he was okay. From that point on, the teasing was different. I think he realized we were friends after all.

Heading to my next class, I heard my name being called from behind. When I turned, I saw Mr. Fern walking toward me.

"Neepa, how are you doing?"

My excitement at knowing that Michael was okay must have remained, making my response more enthusiastic than I intended.

"I am great," I replied.

"Wow, I'm so glad to hear that. Can I walk you to class?"

"Sure."

"Any more issues?"

"Don't even think about mentioning the note," Ego warned.

"No, everything is good."

"Good, good. It seems like you're fitting right in here."

"Thanks. Yes, I'm getting used to this place." Before I entered my class, I turned to him. "Can I ask you something?"

"Sure, what is it?"

"How did you get that limp?"

"Oh, that thing. Nothing special. Just an old baseball injury. I played in college and tore my ACL running the bases. It never healed properly, so that ended my career. Why do you ask? Most people don't even notice?"

"Really? I don't know, I just notice things. So that's why you asked if we like the Cubs or White Sox."

"Yes, my dream was to play for the Cubs. But I found something better, hanging out with people like you."

The next day when Enapay and I boarded the school bus, everyone was buzzing. I looked at him, wondering what was going on. He didn't know any more than I did. Then we overheard a couple of kids talking.

"Yeah, I saw on the news that he jumped in front of a light rail train and was killed instantly."

Enapay interrupted their conversation. "Who jumped?"

"The brother of a girl who goes to our school. I think her name is Leah."

My face drained of all its color.

"Neepa, what's wrong?"

"I know who they're talking about. Leah is in my visual arts class. She reached out to me after she heard T was bothering me, but I shut her down."

When I got to visual arts class, her seat was empty, and Mr. Taylor gave us as much information as he could share. She would not be returning to school for a couple of weeks.

After school, I went to draw in the park. It had been an emotional day, and I needed some downtime. Sitting under my tree, I could hear the beautiful sound of wind chimes from a house nearby. The tone was deep and soft, putting me in a peaceful place. As I looked around to find inspiration, a pinecone fell, hitting me on my head.

"Ouch. What the . . ." I looked up and saw two squirrels running around in the tree. They were young squirrels chasing each other through the branches. Watching them made me laugh, and they didn't seem to notice that I was even there. They were so oblivious that they ran down the trunk of the tree, almost jumping on my head. As they scurried away across the grass, I heard a hawk's cry. I glanced up and saw a magnificent hawk perched at the top of a not-too-distant tree, its white underbelly shining in the sun. The two squirrels also heard the hawk's cry and found safety up the closest tree they could find.

How majestic it looked. It was a redtail perched high, looking at everything below. I stood up to get a closer look at it then it took flight and landed on the ground just a few feet away from me. Not knowing what to do, I froze. Was it hurt, or should I be scared? Our encounter was only a few minutes, until its huge wingspan was on display when it took flight, and I could hear the flap of its wings as it flew away. Now, that had to be a message. I grabbed my stuff and hurried back to the apartment to see if Grandpa had given me a poem about a hawk.

> *Hawk, hawk, your vision is keen.*
>
> *Noticing everything that can be seen.*
>
> *Your cry carries messages to keep me aware.*
>
> *Open my senses to the wisdom that is shared.*

Thinking about the poem, I felt like this had to do with my situation with T. The hawk was telling me I would receive wisdom, and the squirrels were there to remind me that change was coming.

Mom got home earlier than normal and didn't feel like cooking, so we ordered takeout from her new favorite hole in the wall. She had me run in and pick up the empanadas, but before entering, I looked in the window to make sure that T was not around. Luckily, the order was ready, so I was in and out. Exiting, I couldn't see Mom or the car. My phone pinged with a text saying she had to move the car and was waiting around the corner. To reduce the chance of running into T, I rushed to the car. As I approached the alley that led to the back of the restaurant, I felt off and uneasy. There was an odd noise. The closer I got to the alley, the louder the sound. Whatever was going on didn't sound good. Panicking, I passed the alley as quickly as possible, but it didn't feel right. The hairs on my neck were on end. I had to go back. Then I saw it. A man was beating a young woman, swearing at her and kicking her.

"Hey, what are you doing?" I instinctively yelled.

*"What are **you** doing?"* Ego questioned.

The man stopped, and then I noticed the bloodied face of T cowering against the wall. He turned and started walking toward me.

"Why don't you mind your business, bitch!" he exploded.

"Neepa, run!" Ego instructed.

I backed up and pulled out my phone to indicate I was ready to call the police.

"T, are you okay? Do you want me to call the police?" I yelled, keeping an eye on the man.

He smiled as if he knew T wouldn't allow that to happen. He turned back and threw his apron at her. "Clean your face. You can't work like that."

As soon as he left, I ran down the alley to her. She was badly hurt and couldn't stand up. She looked at me. Her eyes were filled with shame.

"T, stay there. I'll call the police."

"No," she blurted from her blood-filled mouth.

"He hurt you. Why? Who is that man?"

"It doesn't matter."

"What?"

"Quiet Girl, just go. Leave me alone. If he gets in trouble, he will beat me worse, plus who will run the shop?"

I didn't know what to do. My phone rang. It was Mom wondering where I was.

"Go. Get out of here," she screamed, spitting blood everywhere.

I felt horrible leaving, but in a weird way, I understood the feeling of embarrassment and shame, like it was her fault she was beaten. When I got to the car, Mom could tell something was wrong. I told her everything, and we agreed that if T was still in the alley when we drove by, we would call the police. She was gone.

Mom knew I was still shaken when we got home.

"Honey, sit down." Immediately, I broke down crying. "What is it?" Mom asked, kneeling in front of me. In between sobs, I told her the girl in the alley was the girl who was bullying me.

"Oh, Neepa. Why didn't you tell me you were being bullied?"

"Because I thought I could handle it, plus you were busy with your new job, Grandma's death, and I didn't want to add any more stress to our lives."

She took my hand. "Honey, I need you to take a breath and tell me everything, from the beginning."

After calming myself, I told Mom the whole sordid list of details. Distraught, Mom mumbled as if she was trying to use her inside voice. "I was so into my world that I didn't even know my own daughter was being bullied and beaten up. What kind of mother am I?" Her lips quivered, shame overwhelming her, and she wept.

"Mom, please. You've always done the best you could. I see that now. I know you were dealing with your own issues trying to keep a roof over our heads. Sometimes things got overwhelming, but look at how things are changing now. Life here is good. You have a great job, and we have friends. You're a great mother. Don't ever question that."

"No, Neepa, I'm supposed to protect and care for you, and I didn't protect you. Does the school know?"

"Yes."

"So why didn't they call me?" Her voice was raw with anger.

"I lied, saying that we didn't want to file a report."

"Neepa, why would you do that?"

"Because it didn't help before, and we usually would be moving by now, so I figured I could just leave it all behind until the next time at the next school."

She got up and paced, becoming more flustered. "But what about the note?"

"I didn't tell them about that because it just happened and there was no proof she wrote it."

Mom tried to hide her anguish, but it didn't work. "Well, it will work this time. Tomorrow, we will file a report."

"No!"

"No? What do you mean, no?"

"I know why she's doing it. It's not me personally. She wants to take her pain and frustration out on someone who is weaker than her, and that is how she sees me, as weak."

"How do you know that?"

"She told me when she was beating me up." We looked at each other in silence.

"So, what do we do now? Who is to say she won't continue to take it out on you?"

"I doubt she will be in school for a few days. Let me handle this my way."

Mom looked at me, not knowing what to do. "I feel horrible because I didn't protect you before, but I don't want to make your life at school any worse. We could leave and move back to Chicago," she suggested.

"No, Mom, I'm tired of running. Please, just let me handle this my way."

Mom looked directly into my eyes. I could see her struggle and pain. "I don't know whether to hug or yell at you, Neepa. Please be careful."

CHAPTER 9

"Hi, Neepa, what brings you in today?"

"Do you have a minute?" I whispered.

She looked around, making sure no one was in earshot. "Of course. Are you okay? Is Tamera bothering you again?" Rachel asked, her voice filled with concern.

"Can we speak in private?"

"Sure, just a second." Rachel gestured for me to follow her into Mr. Fern's office. "He is out at a meeting, so we have time. What's going on?"

"First, I would like to apologize for lying. I told you and Mr. Fern that my mom and I had discussed whether to file a report against T. She didn't know about the incident."

"Is that something you would like to do now?"

"No, but I want to let you know I found out something. You must keep this just between us. Promise?"

Rachel's apprehension was apparent. "It depends on what it is. I can't just make a promise like that."

I turned and walked toward the door, not hiding my disappointment.

"Wait. Neepa, hold up." She paused and let out a sigh. "Against my better judgment, I promise."

I told her about the note, how T thought I was weak, and that I witnessed her being beaten in the alley.

"T needs help. She doesn't need a report filed against her, which could get her thrown out of school. She has a terrible homelife, and she's in pain, physically and emotionally. Unfortunately for me, I was the chosen target. She needs our help."

Rachel stood there, trying to digest it all. "Wow, Neepa. You're a different kind of kid. Personally, I'm having a hard time seeing past the fact that she beat you up. So, what do you propose we do?"

"I would like to talk to her again when she returns to school, if she does."

"How do you know she won't try to take it out on you again?"

"I don't, but I need to take that chance. If she hurts me again, I promise you, I *will* file a report, but if she doesn't, then I'll need your guidance in finding her help."

"Does your mother know what is going on?"

"Yes, I told her everything and asked that she let me handle it."

"Okay." Rachael searched my face and then gave me a supportive smile. "Here's my cell number. Let me know what you need from me, and please be careful."

"I will. Thank you."

"No, thank you. You truly are special."

Something was changing in me. The need to help T get out of her situation was a giant leap outside of my comfort zone. For some reason, it felt right; in a weird way, helping her was helping me.

T wasn't at school for over a week, allowing things to get back to a semi-normal state for me. However, I needed to figure out a plan to speak with T without getting punched in the face again. The only person who I thought might help was Ann. She might not like it, but she and I would need to trust each other.

Mom's late-night work routine was back in full swing, so I had lots of alone time to figure out my next steps. Grandpa normally came to me in my dreams, but one evening, while I was reading, I heard the call of an owl, and it brought back a memory of when he and I camped out in our backyard in Chicago. Between Grandpa's stories and my five-year-old wild imagination, it truly felt like we were in the middle of the forest. Closing my eyes, I basked in the memory.

"Butterfly, why are you troubled?"

"Grandpa, so much has happened since we last spoke."

"I know, but your wisdom is serving you well. Like the owl, you cannot be deceived. Trust what you know to be true."

"Owl? Grandpa, what do you mean, like the owl?"

The sound of my book hitting the floor startled me from my daydream, and then I heard the owl call again, and I knew it was from Grandpa. *There must be a poem in the shoebox.* Searching, I found a picture of Grandpa and me in our back-yard in Chicago, standing next to a little pup tent. My heart ached for him, but the joy from the memory and his visit gave me peace. Then I found the poem.

Owl, owl, flying silently in the night.

Illuminating the truth that has been kept from other's sight.

True wisdom does not allow you to be deceived.

Show me the reality so I know what to believe.

It seemed like Grandpa agreed I was on the right path. I just wished he guided me on how to get Ann to trust and work with me. A few days later, when Enapay and I were get-ting off the bus, Rebecca ran up to us.

"Hate to break the news to you, but she's back."

A shiver ran down my spine, but I was confident in what I had to do. Enapay looked at me.

"You okay?"

"Couldn't be better," I said with a mischievous smirk.

"Neepa, what are you up to?"

"Nothing. This is going to stop one way or another," I re-plied as I walked into the school, leaving Rebecca and Enapay standing there looking at each other.

My goal was to get to history class without running into T. I got in early and dropped a note on Ann's desk as I passed by. She quickly grabbed it and put it in her pocket. Immediately after school, I headed to the greenbelt park to meet Ann. Or at least I hoped to meet her. I took a seat under my tree and waited, trying to gather my thoughts.

After about fifteen minutes, Ego chimed in, *"This isn't going to happen."*

When I stood to leave, I noticed Ann walking down the path, slowly looking around to find me. Poking out from under the tree, I waved her over.

"Thanks for meeting me here."

"What is going on? If anyone sees me talking to you—"

"I know, I know. Look, I know what is happening to T."

"What do you mean, happening to T?"

"Her life outside of school. I saw her get beat up by a guy behind the restaurant where she works."

"Her stepfather?" Ann asked with concern.

"I think so. I heard him beating her in the alley. When I passed, I yelled at him to stop."

"You did what? Are you crazy?"

"Well, he was beating the crap out of her. I had to do something. When I asked who he was, she said it didn't matter, but if he got into trouble, he would beat her worse and who would run the shop?"

Ann's face dropped. "I knew she was having a hard time at home, but I didn't think it was this bad."

"I know she's taking out her frustration on me, but after this, I'm more concerned for her than for myself. I want to help her."

"What? Why would you do that? She beat you up."

"Well, it's like you said. She doesn't care about me, so it's not personal. She wants to feel like she has some control or power over something in her life."

"Geez, Quiet Girl, you're either crazy or I don't know what."

Neepa bristled at being called quiet girl. In the past, she had been proud to stay quiet. Now, there was a growing desire to have her voice heard. Grandma's words rang strongly in her head about how hard their ancestors fought to be heard, and she was not going to let their sacrifices be in vain.

"Thanks? I think. The reason I asked you to meet me was to figure out a plan to help her. You're her friend, right?"

"Yes, but she's been so off lately that I've kept my distance. It's not like we have sleepovers."

"But you're still on speaking terms?"

"Yes, we are, but how are you going to help her without getting the crap beat out of you?"

"That's why I need your help, but we have to trust each other."

"Ha. Why would you trust me?" Ann questioned.

"I could tell you didn't agree with her beating me up. Kicking books is one thing, but hurting someone is something completely different. I don't believe you want to hurt any-one."

Ann looked at me. "So, what's your plan?"

"All I need you to do is get T to meet me tomorrow in the same bathroom where she beat me up, ten minutes before lunch ends, and to get her to promise that she won't try to hurt me again. Also, I need you to give her this." I handed Ann a sealed envelope. "Do you promise you will do this for me?"

"And how am I going to explain why I'm talking to you?"

"Since we have the same history class, just tell her we're working on a project together. So, do you promise?"

Ann looked down at the envelope and then back at me. "Yeah, sure, I promise."

That night, I could barely sleep. When Mom came home, I was already in bed with the covers over my head. I didn't need to speak with her, and I didn't want to get caught up thinking about what she was up to. The next morning, I was up and out of the house early. When Enapay got to the bus stop, I was already there.

"Wow, why are you out here so early?"

"Remember how I told you that this will all end one way or the other? Well, today is the day."

"What are you going to do?"

"I'm either going to make a friend or I'll get beat up. And if the latter happens, I promise to tell your mom."

"So, you're not going to tell me anything?"

"Nope. I don't want you to get into any trouble. It's safer if you don't know."

"Safer?" Enapay exclaimed.

The morning went by quickly. When the bell rang for lunch, I could feel my heart rate increase. I did the normal routine, got to the lunch table before Enapay, Rebecca, and Julie, and pretended to eat my lunch. I figured it was better to have an empty stomach if I was going to get punched in it and puke everywhere. My hands were sweating as I watched the clock.

"Neepa, is everything okay?" Julie asked.

"Yeah, why?"

"Well, you seem distracted, and you're not eating your lunch. Are you sure you're okay?"

"Actually, my stomach is bothering me. I need to hit the restroom before class. I'll see you all later."

Before anyone could respond, I was standing and walking out of the cafeteria. My adrenaline was pumping, and I could hardly contain myself. Fear and nervousness consumed me. Thank goodness I wore a jacket, as I had completely pitted out my T-shirt. When I got to the bathroom, I slowly opened the door, keeping my guard up. T was leaning against the wall.

"What is this all about, Quiet Girl?"

"First, do you promise not to beat me up?" I asked.

"Yeah, yeah, it's your lucky day," she replied smugly. "Why am I here, and why are you writing me poems?"

"I didn't write the poem. My grandfather did, and I need to talk to you."

"About what?"

"The alley."

T's body stiffened. She walked toward me. "Did you tell anyone about what you saw?" Her tone was threatening.

"Get ready to run," Ego advised.

I backed up and lied. "No, I didn't tell anyone. But I wanted to talk to you about it."

"There is nothing to talk about."

"T, he hurt you."

"It isn't anything that I haven't been through before."

"You know you don't have to live like that."

"Quiet Girl, what do you know? You don't know me. You don't know anything about me."

"I know you bully and beat me up because you're looking to have some kind of control in your life. To feel you have power."

T took another step closer, wincing in pain, and grabbed her ribs. "I mess with you because it's fun," she scoffed.

"How is that any different from what your father is doing to you?"

"Stepfather! And you don't know what you're talking about. I didn't do what I was supposed to do and . . ." she trailed off.

"And he disciplined you by punching you in the face."

"Shut up before I do the same to you." We stood in silence. Finally, T threw the envelope at me. "What is this about?"

I picked up the envelope, pulled out the poem, and read it out loud.

"Snake, snake, your bite is feared.
Delivering your poison like a spear.
You shed your skin to survive.
Teach me to transmute so I may be revived.

"What it means is that you can change your circumstances. The snake sheds its skin and becomes new again. You don't have to live this life."

"Whatever, and who is going to help me?"

"Me."

T burst out laughing, grabbing her ribs in pain. After a few deep breaths, she responded. "Oh yeah, you're going to get my stepfather to stop beating me and my mother."

"Well, maybe I can't do that exactly, but I can be your friend and help you find resources so you and your mom can be safe."

"Look, I don't want you as a friend, and I don't need your help."

"Fine, but just remember who stopped your stepdad from doing much worse." I put the poem back into the envelope and threw it back at T. "I think you still need this, and there is a number on the back that you can call to get some help."

"Can we get out of here?" Ego pleaded.

I turned and walked out. As soon as I was on the other side of the door, I ran down the hall to my next class. Luckily, I made it to history before Ms. Jones locked the door. When I passed Ann, she looked at me as if to ask how it went. I gave a quick head nod and sat in my seat.

On the bus ride home, I was more talkative than usual. All the adrenaline, fear, and anxiousness poured out of me. Enapay knew better than to ask what happened, but he understood that whatever took place was good, plus I didn't have a black eye. Once home, I texted Rachel to let her know that I gave T the school safety helpline, so she shouldn't be surprised if she called. I felt really proud of myself for having the courage to step up to T but also to give her options, which is something you don't think you have if you are being bullied or abused.

CHAPTER 10

Back at school, I didn't worry as much about T, and my newfound confidence spilled into other areas at school and my social life. In English class, I raised my hand to give my interpretation of the emotional conflict Marlow, the main character, had in the *Heart of Darkness*, trying to justify imperialism. The class, including Mr. Wright, seemed to be surprised by my answer. Either because I volunteered to speak in front of the class, which I hadn't done to this point, or because my answer was so insightful.

In the end, it didn't matter. I received a look of approval from Mr. Wright, and Michael gave me a high five as I was exiting the class. There was a part of me that finally felt like I was coming into my own. Things were looking up for us. Mom was doing great at her job; I was letting down my walls and coming out of my shell. There were even kids at school who I classified as friends. Colorado felt like home.

The next day in visual arts, I noticed Leah sitting in the back of the class. She had been quiet since returning to school, and I had been too ashamed of how I had treated her months earlier to speak to her. However, I needed to make things right. As I approached her, she gave me a disdained glare.

"Leah, I'm sorry for acting the way I did when you spoke to me back when T was bullying me. It was completely insensitive of me to have told you to mind your own business when you were just trying to be friendly. Please forgive me, and I'm so sorry about your brother."

Leah looked at me, her eyes probing to see if I was for real. Finally, she admitted,

"No one has ever apologized to me like that before. That really took guts. What you said before hurt, but I can understand why you would act out that way."

In a cringed voice, I asked, "Apology accepted?"

"Yeah, apology accepted."

I didn't want to push things, even though I was curious to see how she was doing, so I left it at that and returned to my seat. When the bell rang, Leah caught me before I headed to my next class.

"Neepa, um, I was wondering if we could talk sometime?"

"Sure, about what?"

She paused and looked up as if she was searching for something. "My brother and what he was going through. Not that I had a lot of friends before he died, but now people are treating me like I have the plague. You are the only person who has given condolences. I just need someone to talk to."

"Of course. I can meet you after school today."

"Really?"

"Yeah. Want to grab a snack at the bakery?"

"Yes, that would be great."

"It might take me a few to get there since I have to take the bus."

"Don't worry, I have a car. Meet you in front of the school, and we can drive there. I'll be in a white Subaru."

"Cool. See you then."

"*Nice work. I guess you are not such a jerk after all,*" Ego complimented.

There were so many kids everywhere, making it seem like the entire high school was hanging out at the shops. Because it was so crowded and noisy at the bakery, I suggested we grab a snack and then go to my spot in the greenbelt near my house to talk. She parked the car on the street, and I led her through the park to the tree that I liked to sit under.

"Is this good? This is where I always come to think and draw."

"Yes, this is great, and this tree is amazing."

"I know. It makes me feel protected." Before devouring my double chocolate brownie, I said, "So, what did you want to talk about?"

Leah picked at the top of her muffin like a bird then finally said, "My brother died by suicide because he was being bullied, and I want to understand what could have been going through his head."

"But I thought he was already in college."

"He was. Bullying just doesn't happen to middle or high school kids."

"Sorry, that was stupid of me to say," I admitted.

"No, many people think that way and can't understand. They just think it happens to young kids."

I took another bite of my brownie and then launched into my history with bullying. "Well, I've been bullied my entire life. We were always moving, and I was always the new kid. I didn't speak much, so I was the perfect target."

"How did you deal with it?"

"Ha, I don't know if you could say that I dealt with it. The first time it happened, I told my mom, and we brought it to the school's attention. The physical part stopped, but they found other ways to make my life horrible—whispering, laughing, and finger-pointing. Even worse was when they acted over-the-top nice, to make me think they wanted to be my friend just so they could dis me later. One good thing about moving so often was I knew that the bullying would stop because we would leave. Unfortunately, the same thing happened at the next school and the next. I stopped telling my mom since she or the school couldn't do anything, and I just lived with it," I explained.

"I think that is how my brother felt. No one could do anything."

"Yes, it gets lonely, and you feel you are in a dark tunnel with no end in sight. You get tired of complaining because grown-ups don't hear you, anyway. You just want to shrink and blend in with the wall so no one notices you. That is why I didn't talk unless I had to. Then the inside bully creeps in."

"Inside bully?"

"Yes, you hear all the bad things for so long, you believe them. You believe there is something wrong with you, that you're not capable or worthy of friendship or love. That's the worst part because it stays with you. If a group of kids laugh, you assume they're laughing at you. It really messes with your head."

"No wonder."

"What?"

"No wonder my brother stopped. He was so gifted. He dreamt of writing a novel. We would talk about it all the time then one day we stopped. He said he couldn't do it, that he wasn't talented enough, and we never discussed it again."

"Yes, you lose your self-confidence."

"So, what's made it different this time? How did you get T to stop bullying you?"

"I realized she wasn't bullying me as a person, but what I represented to her—her own weakness that couldn't stop the violence in her out-of-control homelife. To take back control and not see herself as weak, she took it out on me. If she could control me, then she felt she had control over her life. When you are abused or bullied, the person being bullied is not the problem; it is the person who's doing the harm that has the issues. It's their demons, traumas, and fears that cause them to do those horrible acts. They're spewing all that negative emotion, and I carried the burden. It's not my fault or my issue. However, that really doesn't matter when you're getting beaten or tormented. You can't hear that. All you want is for it to stop."

"But what did you do to get T to stop?"

"I witnessed a horrible act being done to her, and I came to her aid. I took a chance and alerted her to resources so she could get help."

"Wow. That took some guts."

"I don't know about that, but I didn't see her as the bully anymore in that moment. All I saw was a person who needed help."

We sat in silence. Leah's head hung then I noticed tears rolling down her face.

"Hey, hey are you okay?"

"Yeah, I seem to cry all the time now." There was a long pause. "I just wish my brother had had someone in his life like you. Someone who could have helped him. I miss him so much; he was my best friend."

"My grandmother recently passed, so I feel your pain. She was very special to me, but I still talk to both her and my dead grandfather."

"You do what?"

"I talk to them in my dreams."

Leah looked away and her body got tense.

"I'm sorry. Did I make you uncomfortable?"

She didn't respond immediately then under her breath, she said, "The night that my brother passed I dreamt about him."

My smile gave her some confidence to continue.

"He didn't talk to me, but it was wonderful to see his face."

"Before my grandma died, she told me that my grandfather who died a few years ago was always with me. His spirit was with me. I didn't understand until he came to me in my dreams. Now, I regularly speak with him, and he helps guide me through life. What I do is if I have a question or problem before I go to sleep, I ask that my grandfather come to me in my dreams, and he does. You should try it."

Leah's silence made it seem that she was contemplating what I'd told her. Just then, a light breeze blew through. I looked around smiling, feeling my grandfather's presence.

"Neepa, I knew there was something different about you when I first saw you in visual arts class. I'm glad I took the chance and spoke to you."

"Leah, I'm glad you did as well. Even though I was a jerk to you."

She laughed. "Don't worry, you're certainly not one now."

PUPA

The caterpillar will break down on a cellular level
and then reorganize itself into a new form.

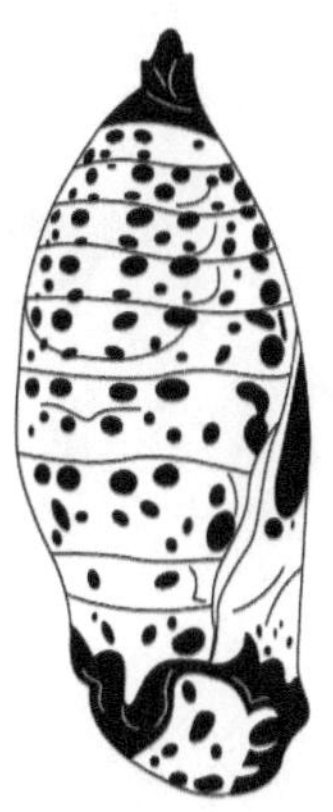

CHAPTER 11

When I came home from school, Mom was sitting at the table.

"Hi. Why are you home so early?"

Mom's face was sullen. No response.

"Mom, why are you here?" I asked again, my voice now filled with fear.

"Neepa, I need to tell you something."

"Is everything okay?"

Mom looked down and became quiet.

"Mom, is everything okay?" My voice sounded panicked.

"I lost my job."

"What?"

"Two weeks ago," she blurted.

"What? Two weeks?"

She didn't respond.

"Where have you been going all this time?"

"Interviewing for other positions."

"Why didn't you tell me?"

She just shook her head.

It killed me to see my mother like this. Before my eyes, she turned from a grown woman into a child waiting to be scolded. A clear image of my grandfather and the rabbit entered my mind.

"See what you did?" Ego accused. *"You were so scared that you made this happen."*

I gave my head a good shake to shut out Ego then I put my bag down and walked over to Mom, wrapping her in a hug. She broke down in tears. I tried to comfort her as best I could. Quietly, I asked, "So what happened?"

"He was married, his wife found out, and I was thrown away . . . again."

Mom cried in my arms like a baby. Mom had never shown this much emotion, and it made me nervous.

"Great, now what do we do?" Ego concluded.

Ego wasn't wrong. There was a pattern. In the past, when this happened, we had to move back to Chicago because Mom couldn't find another job. But this time, it had to be different. "Don't worry, Mom, we will figure this out," I tried to convince her.

"Neepa, I'm exhausted, and so tired of being thrown away. Why can't I find a man to love me?"

Slowly, I began rocking back and forth, trying to comfort Mom as I gathered my thoughts. Mom had grown since we moved to Denver, but one thing still stayed the same: she believed she needed a man. Being the age now that she was when she had me, I realized it must have been really hard for her. Not being able to do what she wanted, like go to college or even graduate from high school, had taken its toll on her. I knew what I had to say to her, but I didn't want to hurt her.

"Mom, you haven't found a man to love you because you don't truly love yourself." Her body winced, as if I'd just stabbed her in the back with a knife. "Mom, you are a beautiful and smart woman, but you go after men only for their money, instead of who they are on the inside. I know you didn't live the life you wanted to live because you had me, and it feels like you are ashamed of your life—like you don't deserve anything nice or a man who truly loves you. Once you decide to love yourself as you are, there will be someone who will love you for you." Gradually, Mom's crying subsided. I could feel life coming back into her body.

"When did you get so grown up and wise?" she whispered.

"Grandpa has been guiding me," I admitted. "Grandma and Grandpa come to me in my dreams."

Mom looked at me, her bloodshot eyes filled with pain. It wasn't because of the job or the guy; it was because they didn't come to her in her dreams.

"Mom, remember how you told me that Grandma and Grandpa are always with us?"

"Yes."

"Well, they have been waiting to unite with you. The shame, worry, and fear you carry have blocked your ability to connect with them. Forgive yourself, be open, and ask them to come to you."

Mom sat up, wiped her tears, and cupped my face in her hands. It seemed like a wave of relief came over her.

"My beautiful, wise daughter. They always knew you were special. Thank you."

"For what?"

"For allowing me to be your mother."

We hugged in silence.

"So, what do we do now?" I asked.

"We're okay for a little while, but . . ."

"But what?"

"My skill set is limited. With only a GED, it's hard to find a good-paying job."

"Well, why don't you go back to school?"

"School? I'm too old for that."

"Really, Mom? You think you're too old . . . or are you scared?"

"Whoa, whoa, watch yourself. I'm still your mother."

"I know," I replied in an apologetic tone. "But you're not too old, so it has to be something else." I kept Mom's stare. Finally, I asked, "What type of job would you like to have?"

"Neepa, we don't have the money for me to go back to school."

"Mom, remember we have the house. Either we can move back to Chicago so we don't have to pay rent and you can take classes online, or we sell, buy something small here, and then you can go to school."

"Wow, you have really thought this out, haven't you?"

"It has crossed my mind from time to time," I replied with a smile. "You have always taught me to be strong and stand on my own. Now, I'm saying that to you. We can do this." I corrected myself. "No, you can do this." Remembering the strength I received from the bear carving the elder gave me at Grandma's funeral, I knew Mom could use it. I got up, walked over to the bed, and pulled out the box that Grandma had given me. Carefully, I unwrapped the bear carving and put it in Mom's hand. "Take this. It will help give you the strength you need to move forward."

Mom's eyes widened. "Where did you find this?" Her voice was flustered.

"I didn't. An elder at Grandma's funeral gave it to me. She said that Grandma wanted me to have it."

Mom ran her finger over the smooth carving, and her eyes welled up with tears.

"What is it? What's wrong?" I asked.

"This fetish used to be mine. Ma gave it to me when I found out that I was pregnant with you. In a fit of anger, I threw it and never thought about it again. She kept it all these years."

"Maybe she knew you would need it again one day."

"Maybe she did. When the elder gave it to you, did she say anything else?"

"She said something about giving me the strength to accept my power."

Mom smiled. "Of course."

"What? What does this all mean?" I asked.

"Grandpa and Grandma always believed you could see and knew things that others could not. They believed I had that gift as well." Mom looked at me intently. "Have you ever just known something about someone else or sensed that something was going to happen?"

I thought for a moment, then I remembered Grandpa's words about my superpower, my spidey sense, and how I could feel Michael's pain and danger from T. Slowly, I nodded my head.

"And were you right?"

"Yes."

"Neepa, this is your gift. It's your intuition, and you're not afraid to use it. But I believe you have even more gifts. You can feel others' pain and emotions, their energy. I used to have intuition, but I was scared and pushed it away. That is why I threw the fetish. I didn't want anything to do with it. Your grandparents knew you had it as well and always hoped that you would accept your gift. You are stronger than me, Neepa. I do hope you choose to accept your gift."

"I didn't understand when Grandpa said it."

"Said what?"

"Grandpa told me a while ago that I had intuition, but I didn't understand."

"Now that you do, ask him, and he'll guide you in how to use it," Mom assured.

That evening, before I fell asleep, I invited Grandpa to come to me.

"Butterfly, you rang?" he said with a cheeky smile.

"Grandpa, you said I have intuition, but what do I do with it?"

"It can help guide you through your life. You don't always have to ask us for guidance. You have your own answers inside you. Quiet your mind and listen to your heart. That is where you will find your answers, where your intuition lies. The more you trust it, the more it grows."

"Does Mom still have it as well?"

"Everyone has this gift, but you must use it and trust it, for it to grow. If not, it will go dormant."

"Grandpa, I love you so much. I won't ever get used to not having you physically with me."

"Losing the physical is hard. We come to earth to experience the physical. Enjoy what you have. Touch, smell, see, hear, taste it all. Use all your senses and know I can be felt in each and every one of them. Butterfly, I am always with you."

It was nice having Mom around more. She was there when I got back from school, something that hadn't happened since I was little. She asked about my day and discovered fresh vegetables. Mom even downloaded some recipes to cook. Unfortunately, the job search was slim, and I could tell she was getting anxious.

At dinner, I asked, "Mom, if you could do anything for a career, what would it be?"

"Ha, I don't know. Never thought about that before."

"Come on, you must have had a dream. What did you want to do before you had me?"

"Wow, that's so long ago." She paused. "I know this doesn't sound sexy, but I wanted to be an economist."

"Really? That would be so cool. What else?"

"You're going to think I'm such a nerd, but since I'm good with numbers, I also thought about becoming an accountant or bookkeeper."

"What about a bank teller?"

"Hmm, never thought about that. I'm sure I could do it."

"I know you could do it. At school, I heard there are kids who are applying to intern at different banks for this coming summer. They have programs to train. Would you consider something like that?"

"Neepa, I'm too old for an internship."

"Come on, Mom, you need to think outside the box. I don't want to move back to Chicago. We need to find you a job here. Josie could find out who will be coming to the school to recruit. Maybe she could help you."

"Okay, Neepa. Let me think about it. In the meantime, I'll go back to the temp agency to see if they have anything."

"Mom, I'm proud of you."

"For what?"

"You are finally allowing yourself to dream."

After school, I asked Enapay if I could come over to speak with his mom.

"Sure, she should be around."

When we walked in the door, he yelled up the stairs, "Mom, I'm home and Neepa is here. She wants to speak with you." He then looked at me and asked, "Do you want a snack?"

"Please." I followed him into the kitchen and hopped up on a stool at the island. Their house was so big. It seemed like our entire apartment could fit into the kitchen.

Enapay walked over to the pantry and asked, "We have granola bars, chips, and fruit. What's your poison?"

"Can I have a granola bar?"

"Coming right up." He turned and slid it across the is-land like he was a bartender in an old western movie.

Then I heard, "Neepa, long time no see. I miss seeing you. How is that possible when you live just downstairs? How's school going?"

"Really good."

"Really?" her voice was filled with intrigue. She took a seat next to me at the island. "So, tell me everything."

In between bites, I told her the entire story about T and how I got her to stop bullying me. I could hear Enapay over at the kitchen table say, "No way!" when I got to the part about the snake poem and meeting T in the bathroom.

"Neepa, I'm so proud of you. I can tell there has been a tremendous weight lifted off your back. What did your mother say?"

"She was happy that she trusted me to handle it my way."

"Great, so how can I help you?"

"Actually, I'm hoping you can help Mom."

"Why? What's wrong?"

"She needs a new job, one that she will be happy at so she can turn it into an actual career."

"I heard about what happened at the architectural firm." Her eyes showed she knew the actual story. "But she said she would go to a temp agency to find something new."

"Yes, but she needs a genuine change, a place where she will thrive."

"It seems like you have something in mind?"

"Well, when I asked her what she thought about doing before she had me, she said an economist, accountant, or bookkeeper. I asked her about the banking industry, and becoming a bank teller, and she said she would be interested. There are kids at school who are applying to intern at banks this summer to learn the business. I thought she could start off as a bank teller and then work her way up as she got more experience. We can't afford for her to go back to school just yet, so I thought this would be a great start, plus if you work for a bank long enough, they help to pay for school."

"Hmm, you really did your homework."

I lowered my head to hide my embarrassment. "Josie, I like it here in Colorado, and I don't want to go back to Chicago. Plus, my mom deserves a good job and, in time, a good man."

"Neepa, I swear you are a wise old soul, and your mom is so lucky to have you looking out for her. Let me look into this. Obviously, she would have to take a different route than a high school kid, but I have connections with the school counselors, and I'm sure they could give me a contact at the banks who recruit at the school."

"Thank you so much, Josie. I just don't want Mom to get caught up in a dead-end job and feel worse about herself than she already does. Can we keep this quiet until you have all the information?"

"Of course."

"I don't want her to make any excuses."

"Got it. I'll let you know what I find out."

"Thanks, and thank you for trusting me and not telling Mom about me being bullied by T."

"Most sixteen-year-old kids don't really know what they're doing, but you surely do. Glad I could support you."

I jumped off my stool and gave Josie an enormous hug, then I turned and said my goodbyes to Enapay. Before I closed the front door, I heard Josie say, "Wow, she is really blossoming into an amazing woman. Are you interested in her?"

"Really, Mom? Why would you ask that? We're just friends."

"Just curious."

It didn't seem long before Josie got back to me with information on how Mom could apply for a bank position. Her connections go deep, and she's very persuasive, so I shouldn't have been surprised. Mom had to supply a resume and references. Hopefully, the architectural firm would do right by her and give Mom a good one. I went to my guidance counselor to see if she could review Mom's resume since she did it for seniors all the time. At first, she was hesitant, but Rachel put in a good word for me, and she agreed to do it. Everything was coming together. Now all I had to do was get Mom to agree.

At dinner, Mom was short-tempered, complaining about all the water around the bathroom sink and frustrated that I'd left a dirty towel on the floor. It had been almost a month since she had a job, and money was getting tight. Just before I cleared the table, I said, "Mom, do you remember when I asked you what your dream job would be?" I took her plate and mine and brought them over to the sink.

"Yes."

"Well, I did some research, and with Josie's help—"

"Josie?"

"Yes, with Josie's help, we found out that the local bank is hiring for teller positions. She has a contact with their human resources department. To apply, all you need is your resume, diploma, or GED credential. If all goes well, and I'm sure that it will, you interview and get the job."

"Whoa, whoa, Neepa. Not so fast."

"Mom, they're paying twenty-two dollars an hour. They give great benefits, and they help pay for college after a certain number of years."

She sat there listening, then said, "I don't have a resume."

"Oh, don't worry, I can help with that, and my guidance counselor said she would review it before you submit it."

"What about references? My former boss at the architectural firm won't give me a reference."

"You just give them the human resources department and, by law, all they can say is that you worked there. They don't go into details, and Josie can be a personal reference."

Mom sat there with a look of astonishment. "Neepa, you have this all planned out."

"Yes, I do. Mom, it's time you did something for you. You are crazy smart, strappy, and a wiz with numbers. This should be a cakewalk for you, and there is so much opportunity to grow. Plus, I really don't want to move back to Chicago. There is nothing for us there. I like it here, and I finally have friends. Will you do it?"

She hesitated. "I don't know, Neepa."

"Mom, you deserve this. We deserve this."

By this time, I had moved from the sink and was almost on top of her at the table, giving her my best puppy dog eyes.

"Okay, okay. I'll do it."

"YES!!" I yelled. "We can start on your resume tonight."

We made a night of it. Josie and Enapay came down and brought some ice cream, and we sat around the table writing Mom's resume. There was so much laughter and joy. For the first time in a long time, I saw Mom happy and carefree.

That night when we got into bed, Mom gave me a wonderful hug.

"Thank you, Neepa."

"It's nothing more than what you would do for me."

"Yes, but I'm supposed to be the mother taking care of you."

"Mom, we have always figured things out together, and that is how it will always be."

She kissed me on the cheek then I watched her quickly fall asleep. She looked so peaceful. When I finally fell asleep, both Grandma and Grandpa greeted me in my dream. They looked so happy.

"Butterfly, you're growing into such a wise woman, and we're so proud of you," Grandpa said as he squeezed me tight.

"Neepa, you have been able to do what I always wanted to do for your mother. Help her believe in herself. She will waver, but stay strong with her, Grandma instructed, smiling at me.

"Don't worry, Grandma, I know she can do this, and I know she'll advance quickly. I believe in her."

"Remind her of the grasshopper, my butterfly. You have a good life in Colorado,"

Grandpa pointed out.

"Yes, we do."

"Then stay. Sell the house in Chicago. There is nothing there for you anymore. You and your mother are creating a new life. I can see Colorado has been good for you. You're growing and opening yourself up, trusting others. We know your mother has mixed feelings, but encourage her to break free of the past. The memories will always be with her, but it's time for her to live her life," Grandma added.

The alarm startled me out of my dream. I rolled over to see Mom sitting at the kitchen table, watching me.

"Good morning, Neepa."

"Morning, Mom. Did you sleep?" My voice was dry and scratchy.

"Yes, very soundly. I have a sense of calm and know that everything will work out. Plus, I had the most wonderful dream. Your grandparents came to me."

"Really?"

"Funny enough, they said for me to trust you, and you would lead us through this next stage in our life."

Just as Mom said that, it reminded me of the grasshopper. I reached under the bed and pulled out the shoebox.

"What is that?" Mom asked as she joined me on the bed.

"Grandma gave it to me when we left Chicago. It has poems, pictures, and other things that she wanted me to have." I searched through the envelope and found the grasshopper poem. "Grandpa asked that I share this with you." I handed her the piece of paper.

Grasshopper, grasshopper, your legs are strong.
The courage you have is something I long.
Unsure of the next step I may take.
Guide me on this leap of faith.

She studied it, and a tear spilled from her eye.

"What's wrong?" I asked.

"Your grandfather always believed that nature was there to guide us, and now he has instilled that wisdom in you. I just wish that I had understood a long time ago—then I wouldn't have wasted so much time."

"Mom, things happen when they're supposed to happen. You're ready for this change. You're ready to take this leap of faith, and we'll all be supporting you."

Mom got up on her haunches and pounced on top of me, delivering the best bear hug I have ever felt.

CHAPTER 12

Per Mom, her interview went great, and her references checked out. A week later, she accepted a teller position, and her training would start within a few weeks. In the meantime, they gave her lots of information to study. This was a perfect time for her to go back to Chicago to check up on the house and to clean the rest of it out.

"Mom, I hadn't mentioned this to you before, but the night that Grandma and Grandpa came to both of us in our dreams, they told me it was time to sell the house."

"Wait? They told you that?"

"Yes, they also said you would have some hesitation, but they want us to start a new life here in Colorado."

"Neepa, I don't know. They worked so hard to get that house."

"And it served its purpose. Mom, we have a different life here now. I don't want to go back, do you?"

It's a good thing Mom didn't play poker because she couldn't hide her emotions. Finally, she answered, "No, I don't want to live there either."

"So, when you go back, don't you think it would be a good idea to get with a real estate agent?"

She nodded.

"Just think, Mom, with the money you'll make from the sale, we can buy something small here, and now that you have a full-time job, we can actually create a home for ourselves."

A slight smile appeared on her face.

I couldn't tell if she was happy or if she was responding to my excitement. In the end, I knew this was the right move for us.

The next morning, Mom was up early to head back to Chicago. I walked her out to the car.

"Okay, Neepa, are you sure you'll be okay staying here by yourself?"

"Mom, I'm not by myself. Josie and Enapay are right up-stairs. I'll be fine. Don't worry, and get as much done as you can."

"Yes, I will. Call me if you need anything. I'll have my phone by me all the time."

"Got it, Mom. Drive carefully and text me from the road. I'll call you when I can in between classes. I love you." I gave her a big, smushy hug. She kissed me on the forehead and jumped into the car. I watched as she drove away.

Walking back into the apartment, a wave of loneliness hit me and made me wonder how I would manage when I went to college. Sometimes, it seemed like Mom and I were more like twin sisters than mother and daughter. However, this time apart would be good for us and hopefully would provide Mom with the time she needed to get used to the idea of selling the house.

For the next few days, I spent a lot of time with Josie and Enapay. They invited me to dinner every night, and Enapay and I did homework together. Mom was working hard at the house, donating clothing, housewares, and stuff that we would never use back here in Colorado. She also met with an agent and got an appraisal on the house. My grandparents kept it in good condition, so there were no major repairs that needed to be done. Each time I spoke with Mom, I got the sense that she was actually coming around to the idea of selling it.

Back at school, Leah fit right in with Rebecca, Julie, and Enapay, and when I walked into history class, Ann went out of her way to say hello. I had to check to see if there was a full moon because things were going *almost* too well. Mom would be back the next day, so after school, I took the bus to the store to pick up some food. My eyes were bigger than my wallet, and I found myself five dollars short. I searched through every pocket of my jacket and book bag to find more money, as my face grew redder with the realization that I would have to put something back. Then I felt someone reach over my shoulder and hand the cashier some money. When I looked up, all I saw was the back of a man with a slight limp walk out the door.

"Did he just give you money?" I asked the cashier.

"Yes, he did. Paper or plastic?"

Back at the apartment, I unpacked the groceries and went straight to Grandpa's boxes. Grandpa was not a huge sports fan, but he enjoyed baseball when he got to go. I went to his memorabilia box and poked around. Under some old magazines was a baseball program from a 1971 game between the Cubs and the New York Mets. When I flipped it over, there was an autograph. It was hard to read, but I thought it said "Ernie Banks." I checked the internet and found out that 1971 was the last year Ernie Banks played for the Cubs. He was a Hall of Famer, hitting 512 home runs, and winning the Lou Gehrig Memorial Award. I called Mom to tell her what I had found and asked if I could have it. She didn't care either way since she didn't follow baseball.

Before class the next day at school, I headed down to the administration office.

"Hi, Rachel."

"Neepa, how are you doing?"

"I'm good. Is he in yet?"

"Yes. Do you have an appointment?"

"No, I was hoping I could just grab a few minutes with him."

"Okay, let me check." She walked to his office and then motioned for me to come back.

He smiled as I walked in. "Neepa, how can I help you?"

"Mr. Fern, I wanted to say thank you for yesterday."

"Yesterday, what do you mean?"

"I know that limp anywhere. Thank you for your generosity."

With a coy smile, he said, "It's all I could do for someone who is so giving of herself and willing to help others." The first bell rang, only giving me a few minutes before I would be late to class. "Better get to class," he instructed.

I hesitated briefly, then placed the autographed program on his desk, quickly turned, and headed out. It took a few moments, but I heard him call after me.

"Neepa, wait."

I turned and smiled. "Sorry, can't hear you. Gotta go. Don't want to be late for class."

After school, I went home to prepare Mom a delicious meal. She would arrive around seven o'clock, so I took my time preparing a frozen lasagna, fresh green salad, and store-bought breadsticks. Homework done, house cleaned, and dinner would be ready when she walked in the door. Around seven-thirty, I finally heard her car in the driveway. I ran out to greet her and grab her bags.

"Oh, Neepa, it's so good to see you. I really missed you."

"Missed you, too, Mom. How was the drive?"

"Long and uneventful."

"Good, well, dinner is ready. I hope you're hungry."

"Dinner? What did you make?"

"You'll see."

We grabbed Mom's bags and some things she brought from Grandpa and Grandma's house. When we walked into the apartment, it smelled like an Italian restaurant.

"Neepa. It smells amazing."

"I'll get everything on the table while you wash up."

When she came out, I poured her a glass of wine, and dinner was served.

"Geez, I guess I should go away more often," she laughed.

Halfway through dinner, Mom's phone rang. She looked down, and her face became sober.

"Neepa, I need to take this." She pushed her chair from the table and went into the bathroom. A few minutes later, she walked out.

"Who was that?" I asked.

"Oh, just house stuff," she said sheepishly.

Mom's bank teller training was going well, and each night, we studied and did homework together, sitting at the kitchen table with papers sprawled out around us. As I thought it would, this all came quickly to her. Two weeks into her job, she came home filled with excitement.

"Neepa, I know what I want to do."

"What do you mean, what you want to do?"

"Remember, when you asked what I dreamed about doing before I had you?"

"Yes."

"Well, I changed my mind. I want to be a financial planner."

"A what?"

"A financial planner. They help people budget, create savings strategies, and develop a thorough financial plan."

"Okay, now you're speaking another language."

"In one of my training courses, they discussed different bank jobs, and this really interested me. I particularly want to work with women and single mothers. It will take time, but I have finally figured out what I want to do with my life."

It was impossible to hide my smile, and a warm feeling of pride filled me.

"Mom, remember how Grandma and Grandpa would call me butterfly?"

"Yes, of course."

"Do you know why they did that?"

"I never got a full explanation, but I figured it was because of how beautiful you were . . . are."

"Not exactly." I went into the shoebox and found the butterfly poem and read it out loud to Mom.

> *"Butterfly, butterfly, you have many stages of life.*
> *Your wings catch the air as you take flight.*
> *Transforming from egg, larva, cocoon to final birth.*
> *Guide me through the next step of my journey on this earth.*

"I think it's about time that we started calling you butterfly. It feels to me that you're about to take flight. I know Grandma and Grandpa are so proud of you."

"I hope so."

"Don't hope, just know they are."

Mom completed her training and was a full-fledged bank teller. She had already received recognition from her manager for her knowledgeable service to clients.

Just as I boarded the bus, my phone dinged. Enapay plopped down in the seat next to me. I grabbed my phone and read Mom's text saying that she was going out for drinks with her colleagues. My demeanor changed immediately.

"Here we go again," Ego impulsively stated.

"Hey, what's up? Everything okay?" Enapay asked.

"Yeah, Mom's got a meeting tonight."

"Oh, do you want me to ask if you can join us for dinner?"

"Thanks, but I have to study for our calc exam."

"Oh, snap, thanks for reminding me."

I tried to ignore what Ego had said, but admittedly, it scared me.

Leah ran up to me in visual arts, looking like she was going to pop.

"What's up?" I asked.

"OMG, Neepa, I just got the best news. Well, I think it's great news . . ."

"Leah, what is it?" I urged.

"My family has created a fund at my brother's college in his name to support victims of bullying."

"Wow, that is really awesome."

"Do you think so?"

"Yes, of course. To help others is an amazing thing to do."

"I'm so glad you said that because I wanted to ask you something." She paused.

"What is it? Leah, you're killing me. What is it?"

"Well, the college asked my family to attend an event for National Stop Bullying Month to announce the fund, and I wanted to invite you to attend with us."

"Oh, Leah, that is so nice." I paused.

Leah's face changed. "But I understand if you can't go," she continued.

"I would love to attend with you all."

"Really? Great. I've told my parents so much about you, and they can't wait to meet you."

On the bus ride home, Enapay looked at me. "Neepa, what are you up to?"

"Why do you ask?"

"You have this look on your face. I can't tell what it's about."

"It's pride," I admitted.

"Nice. What's that about?"

"Leah invited me to attend an event with her family to announce a fund they've established at her brother's college."

"Really? That is pretty cool."

"I thought so as well. But I'm proud of myself for saying I would attend. When I first moved here, I would never have accepted an invitation like that, let alone attend an event where I didn't know anyone. I'm proud to say I've come a long way."

"Yes, you have, and you don't roll your eyes at me nearly as much as you used to," Enapay pointed out.

At eight o'clock on the dot, Mom returned home. *It was earlier than her* other *outings, so maybe this was legit*, I thought.

"Hi honey, I'm home," she announced. "How was your day? Did you eat?"

She was in a good mood, giving me the sense that she actually was out with friends. So, I buried my angst. However, there was something. I couldn't exactly put my finger on it, but there was something that just didn't feel right.

"My day was good. I have a test tomorrow in calc, so I have been studying all night, and no, I didn't eat."

"Oh, honey. Let me make you something. I had bar food, so I'm not hungry. Will a grilled cheese work?"

"Yeah, that works. Thanks. So . . ."

"Careful, Neepa, we don't want her to think you don't trust her," Ego cautioned.

"Who were you out with tonight?"

"That's your careful?" Ego questioned.

"Oh, a group from the bank. They go out every Thursday. It's nice to talk with colleagues outside of work. They help me with the ins and outs of the bank."

"Cool. I'm so glad you're making friends."

"You mean you are glad that I'm not up to my old ways?"

My face turned beet red. "Yes, I'm glad about that as well."

"Neepa, I've been doing a lot of thinking, and it's time to sell Grandma and Grandpa's house."

"Really?"

"Yup. Per the real estate agent, it's a good time to sell. I'll need to go back to Chicago one more time to get things ready."

"When will you do that?"

"I don't know. Maybe take a half day next Friday or Monday if my manager will allow it."

"Wow. Okay. Do you want me to come with you?"

"Of course. It'll be the last time we'll be in Chicago for a long time."

I shared the news about Leah and the invitation.

"Neepa, that is wonderful. I assume it's local."

"Yes, she still needs to give me the details, but he went to college in state."

"Seems like we're both making friends," Mom said with a warm smile on her face. "Grandma and Grandpa were right; this is a great place for us to live our lives. Seeing you happy and coming out of your shell gives me great joy."

CHAPTER 13

The tiresome drive back to Chicago seemed to take longer than the last trip. When we entered the house, dragging our feet, it echoed and smelled musty. Seeing it almost empty made me notice things I hadn't seen before, like the house's architecture. Dark wood trim, sturdy stairwell, big front window, and wood floors. It now seemed modest, in comparison to the houses in Denver, at least in the neighborhood where we were living.

Mom had already donated most of the furnishings to the Indian Center. Unfortunately, for us, the old mattresses had been discarded, leaving Mom and me to sleep on an air mattress for the next few days. The bounciness of the mattress made staying asleep almost impossible. Every time Mom rolled over, I was thrown to the floor.

On our first night, Grandpa came to me briefly. "Neepa, remember the blue jay," he said and then recited the poem.

Blue jay, blue jay, how striking are you?
Basking all that sees you in the vibrancy of blue.
Singing loud and proud for all to hear.
Give me confidence to express myself without fear.

Before we even had time to figure out what we'd eat for breakfast, the real estate agent came to the house to discuss the details of putting the house up for sale. None of that interested me, so I asked Mom if I could go down to the neighborhood park where Grandpa and I used to always go.

"Be careful. And hey, we'll finish in an hour, so be back by then."

"Okay, I'll be back soon."

The walk was quiet, and I loved being able to breathe the fresh air outside. I saw a few kids on the swings at the playground with their parents sitting nearby. I planted myself on the bench where Grandpa and I used to sit. From there, I could see across the entire park, including some joggers and people walking their dogs.

The birds were singing, and I got lost in their songs. The blue jay's call cut through the other birdsongs and brought me back to my surroundings.

"Hey, Quiet Girl, is that you?"

I turned and saw two girls walking toward me. At first, I didn't recognize them, then I realized I had gone to elementary school with them. They had not been nice to me, and instantly, a collage of bullying memories ran through my head. As they approached, I realized that bullies rarely act alone. They always have a sidekick. *Why is that?* I wondered.

"What, haven't you learned to speak yet? Oh, I forgot, she's dumb." They looked at each other and laughed.

"Actually, my name is Neepa."

"Oh, excuse us. Didn't know you could speak."

"Can I help you with something?" I asked. They glared at me. "Oh, I see. You thought I would still be scared of you, and you would have some fun."

"What did you say, Quiet Girl?" one replied in a huff.

An energy grew inside me that I had never felt before. I stood up and yelled, *"I said my name is Neepa, can I help you with something? Oh, did you think you could beat me up again?"*

The kids stopped playing, and I could see their parents look our way. The girls also felt the extra attention. They both nervously looked around.

"Nothing to say? Now, who are the quiet girls?"

"Seriously, don't push it," Ego warned.

"Whatever. Let's get out of here. This girl is crazy."

Chest full of pride, I sat back down. That was the first time I had stood up for myself, and it felt amazing. At that moment, the blue jay's call rang in my ears, and I remembered my dream and Grandpa's words. Thank you, Mr. Blue Jay, for giving me the confidence to sing loud and proud without fear.

Returning to the house, Mom was organizing the last few boxes we would bring back with us.

"How was the park?"

"It was great."

"Really?" she asked, with her voice filled with surprise. "Why so?"

"I ran into a couple of girls from elementary school."

"Everything okay?"

"Yeah, it was great."

It had been a long day, and we were hungry, so we went out to find some dinner. The neighborhood had changed a bit since I'd been back. Driving down the street, I noticed a pho restaurant.

"Oh, Mom, do you want some pho?"

"I haven't had it before, but I'm game."

We parked the car and hurriedly walked a block to the restaurant. When we entered, it was full of activity. We noticed a group of people laughing and joking at another table. Seated, Mom and I looked over the menu, when I felt someone staring at us. I glanced up.

"Mom, there is a man at the next table staring at us." When Mom looked up, he said in a heavy foreign accent, "Mina, is that you?"

I looked at Mom and could see the surprise in her face. "Marco, Marco Bernardi?"

"Yes, oh my goodness, it has been so long. You are all grown up . . . and beautiful, I might add." The connection was immediate and strong. Mom blushed.

"Well, you have also grown up. What are you doing here?"

"This is my favorite pho shop."

"Oh, so you still live here in Chicago?"

"Actually, no. Just out here for work. After high school, I went to college in Colorado and stayed."

"Colorado?" Mom and I said in unison.

"Yes, I live in Denver. Why do you both sound so surprised?"

Mom laughed. "Oh, sorry, we also live in Denver."

"Really? So, what are you doing back in Chicago?"

"I lost my mom a few months ago, and we're getting ready to sell my parents' house."

"Oh, I'm so sorry for your loss. Is this your sister?" he asked.

Mom giggled. "No, this is my daughter, Neepa. Neepa, this is Marco, an old friend from high school."

I smiled.

"Neepa, your mother broke my heart when we were young, and I'm sure you are doing the same, as you are just as beautiful."

"Thank you," I said under my breath.

"Mina, I would love to catch up with you back in Denver. May I have your number, or is there a mister who would object?"

Mom chuckled and replied, "That would be really nice, and no, there is no mister." She then took his phone and put in her number. "I guess I should ask if there is a missus who I need to be concerned with."

Okay, now this was getting really uncomfortable for me, but down deep, I was so glad she asked.

"No, too busy with work, but I do have a dog, and she won't mind."

We all laughed.

Before leaving, he took Mom's hand and gave her a kiss on each cheek. "Farfalla, I look forward to seeing you again. Have a nice evening."

Mom smiled and tried to play it off, but I could tell there were some unresolved feelings.

Once he left, I looked at Mom and said, "So . . ."

"So what?" she replied, looking at the menu and trying to act normal, but the twinkle in her eyes said something very different.

"Who is he?" I asked excitedly. "And why did he call you Farfalla?"

"We knew each other in high school. He's originally from Italy, and his family moved to Chicago for his father's work. I don't know why he called me that. It was his nickname for me back in high school."

I grabbed my phone and looked up the word. "Mom, he called you butterfly in Italian."

"Huh, I had no idea that is what it meant."

"So, did you date?"

"We flirted but never went out on a date. Then I got pregnant with you and left school. I hadn't seen him since then."

"Well, *obviously*, he remembers you."

Mom's perm-a-smile lasted the entire evening.

Even though Mom and I were ending this Chicago chapter of our lives, there was an excitement for things to come. Closing the door to Grandma and Grandpa's house was bittersweet, but I knew it was the right thing for us to do. We said our goodbyes to Ms. Brown and invited her to come out and visit anytime. When she hugged Mom, I heard her say, "Know that your parents are very proud of you."

"Thank you. I'm pretty proud of myself as well," Mom replied with a smile.

We packed the car with the last items from the house and took a drive around the neighborhood one last time, then swung by the Indian Center and my old high school. So many memories. Some good and some bad, but they made us who we were. If nothing else, they made us strong and brought Mom and me closer.

"Neepa, once we sell the house, where would you like to live?"

"It would be nice to still be near Enapay and Josie, but if that's not possible, I want to stay at the same high school."

"Don't worry about that, no more new schools for you until college!" Mom exclaimed. "Well, I guess it will come down to how much the house sells for and what we can afford."

"Can I get my own room?"

"Of course. At a minimum, we should have two bedrooms and two bathrooms."

"And a backyard?"

"Sure."

"Can we also have a dishwasher and our own laundry?"

"Done."

"Mom, this is so exciting. I never thought this day would come."

"I know. We've come a long way from finding our stuff out in the street or moving in the middle of the night because we couldn't afford rent." Mom reached over and squeezed my hand. "No more of that for us, young lady."

I put my head against the window and fell asleep with a smile on my face.

We didn't get back to Denver until the early morning. And the next day at school, I was exhausted. My eyes were dry, and I couldn't get hydrated again. I guess my body liked sea level better than being up a mile high. I looked and felt horrible, so I kept an even lower profile than normal. In history class, Ann slipped an envelope to me as I passed to go to my seat. I recognized it as the one I'd given to T. Inside was the snake poem with a note written at the bottom.

Quiet Girl, Mom and I are getting out. Heading to California to live with family. Thanks for opening my eyes and letting me know things can be different. This snake is shedding its skin. T

No wonder I hadn't seen T in school before we left for Chicago. I was concerned, but it wasn't like she and I had become friends. T just stopped bullying me, and if we saw each other in the hall, we gave each other a quick glance. It was more on her part than mine since she had to keep up her tough appearance, and that couldn't happen if she befriended the person she had bullied. I could feel Ann's stare. When I looked up, my eyes were misty, but I had a huge grin on my face. Ann gave me a quick smile, then turned away. A warm sensation came over me and filled me with energy. I could hear Grandma and Grandpa say, "You did good. We are so proud of you. Fly, butterfly, fly."

After school, Josie was on the front porch waiting for Enapay and me, holding a glass vase filled with an enormous flower arrangement of lilies.

"Geez, nice flowers, Mom. Who are they from?" Enapay teased.

"I don't know. They're actually for Mina."

"Mom?" I questioned.

"Yes, seems like she has an admirer."

I didn't know what to think. Josie handed me the flowers, and I saw a small envelope attached to a plastic stem nestled in the bouquet.

"Enapay, help Neepa open the door," Josie instructed.

I carefully carried the vase down to the apartment, the whole time staring at the card. Enapay opened the door and helped me place the arrangement on the table.

"Who do you think they're from?" he asked.

"No clue."

"Well, whoever they're from, he's definitely making it known that he is interested."

After Enapay closed the door to leave, the apartment quickly filled with the scent of lilies. Mom wouldn't be home for another hour, and the temptation to peek at the card was eating me up. I did my best to keep myself preoccupied with homework. But every time I looked up from my work, all I could see was the card.

"Those flowers look expensive; they must be from her old boss," Ego surmised.

"No, don't say that."

"Maybe it's someone new . . . who she had drinks with recently," Ego offered.

"Enough," I said out loud.

"Enough what?" Mom asked as she walked through the door. Then she stopped dead in her tracks. "Neepa, where did you get those amazing flowers?"

"They're not for me; they're for you."

"Me?" Mom squealed. She took in a deep breath. "I love the smell of lilies. How would someone know that?"

"So, you don't know who they're from?"

"No. Should I?"

"Well, there is a card. Read it."

Mom carefully moved aside a few lilies and pulled out the card. She started reading.

"Mom," I whined. "Read it out loud."

"Okay, okay."

Mina, it was an amazing surprise to see you in Chicago. I had almost forgotten how stunning you are. Your beauty reminds me of the lily, the flower of Rome. It represents purity and exquisite beauty. I look forward to when we can see each other again. Marco.

It was as if Mom lost every bone in her body. She melted into the kitchen chair.

"Mom, how did he know where we live?"

"Hmm, that's a good question. Actually, we texted after I saw him with you. I told him we were staying with Josie. In the conversation, I mentioned her husband's death. He remembered hearing about it on the news. I guess he is a good detective."

"Mom, Mom, your phone. It's buzzing."

"Oh, shoot, where is it?" She rummaged through her bag.

"Hello?" A huge smile appeared on her face. "Yes, thank you. The flowers are absolutely gorgeous."

I watched as Mom transformed into a teenage schoolgirl, giggling and blushing. To give her some privacy, I grabbed my coat and went outside to sit on the stoop. Staring off into space, I realized there were only a couple of weeks before Christmas and I still hadn't found a gift to get Mom. I suspected she wasn't thinking about Christmas gifts either. Between getting Grandma and Grandpa's house ready for sale, paying rent, and taking care of other obligations, Mom was still getting back on her feet after not working for a while.

The holiday was going to be lean for the two of us, but I wanted to do something for her. I needed my creative juices to kick in.

Quietly, I asked Grandma what I should get Mom. Instantly, the word "poems" popped into my head. Yes, I can give Mom Grandpa's poems. I could draw the animal and then somehow put the poem with the animal. My visual arts teacher would be the perfect person to help me think this through. Happy with my decision, I stood up and poked my head through the door to see if Mom was done. She waved me in.

"Tomorrow night? Sure. That sounds wonderful. See you then," Mom purred.

"Tomorrow night what?" I asked.

"Marco asked me out to dinner."

"Really? Where are you going?"

"I don't know. He said he would pick me up from work, and it would be a surprise." Mom's smile was infectious. She tried to act cool, but the excitement radiated from her body.

Before the sun was up, Mom was digging through our closet.

"Neepa, quick, help me pick out something to wear." Mom's voice was frantic. "Whatever it is, it has to go with a blazer or sweater, since he will pick me up from work."

I went into the wardrobe and looked through her clothes.

"What about this?" I asked, holding up a gray pencil skirt and a blue patterned silk blouse. "You could wear your blue blazer with it."

"You think so?" Mom questioned.

"It shows enough, but not too much, if you know what I mean." I flashed her a motherly look.

"Yes, I agree. I don't need to show the goods to get a man more interested in me."

My jaw dropped. "Excuse me, did I just hear what I think I heard?"

"Yeah, yeah, yeah. I guess you've been rubbing off on me."

"It's either that or you really like him," I remarked, my face beaming.

"Why are you all smiles?" Mom asked. "You've never been interested in the men I have dated before."

"Because I've never seen you this excited before. With other guys, you used your assets to attract them, and I think deep down, you were not interested in really getting to know them. Marco feels different."

"Well, he was always good to me in high school, and even though I bloomed early, he seemed interested in me and my brain."

My relationship with my mom had fluctuated between mother-daughter and sisterly, but now I felt like I was back to being the mother.

"Well, take it slow. Get to know him," I pleaded. "Remember, we don't *need* a man in our lives, but if you are ready to have one, let's make sure he's a good one."

Mom smiled. "Come here." She pulled me in for a hug. "Do you know I love you?"

"Yes, and I love you too."

"Okay, well, you better get to the bus. I'll text you when I get to the restaurant."

"No, text me when he picks you up, then when you get to the restaurant, and again when you leave. Can't be too careful."

"Alright, *mother*," she replied in a teasing voice.

I ran up the driveway to make sure the bus hadn't already arrived. At the top of the driveway, I heard Enapay yell out the bus window, "Hurry up!" The door was just closing when I threw my book bag in, and I stopped the bus driver from closing the door.

"Nice move," Enapay complimented.

"Phew, that was close. I was helping Mom pick out an outfit for her date tonight, and I lost track of time," I explained.

"Is it the flower guy?"

"Yeah."

"Who is he?"

"I met him briefly when we were back in Chicago. My mom knew him in high school."

"So, you haven't Googled him yet?"

"What do you mean?"

"Seriously, that is the first thing you should do. Who knows who this guy is? Aren't you the least bit curious?"

"Yes, but I hadn't even thought about doing that."

"Really? I guess you don't date much."

"Date? No, I've never been on a date."

Enapay gave me a surprised look. "Really? You have never been on a date? Wow, okay then. Well, now you know for when you do." He tried to cover up his surprise.

"Why are you so surprised?"

"You're sixteen. Even I've been on *one*."

"Well, it's not a big priority of mine. Plus, no one has ever asked me out."

"You probably wouldn't go if they did."

"Why would you say that?"

"It's written all over you. Just like my mom. She's not interested and hasn't dated since my stepdad died, but when she does, I'm going to be all up in that guy's life before she leaves the house."

I sat there in deep thought, wondering what I should do. Mom seemed to trust him, but that didn't mean I couldn't learn a little about him just to be sure he was a good guy.

At lunch, I asked Rebecca, Julie, and Leah what I should do. They all agreed it wouldn't hurt to check up on this guy.

"What's his name?" Leah asked.

"Marco. He is Italian, from Italy."

"Okay, but what is his last name?"

"B something. It's Italian. I don't know."

"Bellini, Bottici, Bongiovanni," Rebecca started hurling names at me.

"How do you know these names?" I asked her.

"They're on the internet."

"Whoops, didn't think of that." I giggled with an embarrassed look on my face.

Finally, Enapay said, "Bernardi."

"That's it!" I exclaimed.

"Bernardi?" Leah asked. "Like the luxury leather line, Bernardi?"

Everyone looked at each other. "Wait, you guys never heard of Bernardi bags?" Leah couldn't understand.

"Sorry, outside of my price range," Julie stated.

"Well, look him up," Enapay urged. All four of us grabbed our phones to search.

"Neepa, is this him?" Leah handed me her phone.

"OMG, it is." I read the description out loud. "Marco Bernardi named CEO of Bernardi Fine Leather Goods USA, a subsidiary of Italy's number three luxury leather bag manufacturer, after the passing of his father, Marco Bernardi, Senior."

"Was that recently?" Enapay asked.

"Two years ago. Wow, that is amazing."

"That's all great, but we need to make sure there is nothing weird about him. Has he been seen with celebrities or been arrested for a DUI?" Enapay asked.

"Geez, Enapay. Can't he just be a good guy?" Julie asked.

"Can't be too careful," he warned.

"Seems like he's clean," Leah stated after a few minutes. "Says here, he has an engineering degree from the University of Colorado and worked for a prestigious engineering firm in Denver."

"Yes, he told us he went to school here and just stayed. He didn't mention the part about being the CEO of a luxury leather line."

"Well, that isn't something you just blurt out," Julie advised.

"True, he seemed like a humble guy. Mom said that he was more interested in her mind than her digits in school." I fell back in my seat as a wave of relief washed over me. "Phew."

"Hey, Neepa, did you see that his company also has a foundation for underserved communities in Chicago? Check this out. Serving and supporting the diversity of Chicago through scholarships, internships, and mentorship for young people wanting to make a difference."

"Wow, I like him already. He definitely made an impression on Mom, and he's making one on me as well."

"If this works out for them, please let him know I'm a huge fan of his work," Leah commented.

Enapay invited me up for dinner, since Mom was on her date. We also studied for our biology quiz. Mom texted as requested, and at nine o'clock I headed back down to the apartment, knowing she would be home soon. Not soon after I entered the apartment, I heard her car pull into the driveway. Quickly, I ran over to the couch and pretended that I was reading.

"Home so early?" I asked casually when she stepped through the door. Mom floated across the room with an enormous smile on her face.

"Good date?"

"Beautiful."

"Beautiful?" I questioned.

"He is a beautiful person. So peaceful and grounded. Exactly how I remembered him."

"Are you going to see him again?"

"Yes. I hope so."

"What do you mean, hope?"

"I told him you asked that we take this slowly."

"You did what?" I shrieked.

"Yes, I did, and he understood and agreed."

"Oh, okay."

"And he wanted me to give this to you."

"What is it?" Mom handed me a bag with the name Bernardi written in gold across the front. A brown box with a gold ribbon held a beautiful leather zip wallet with my initials embossed in gold in the lower right corner. The fragrance of the leather reminded me of when I was young, back in Chicago. Grandpa always wore a leather pouch around his neck that held special things, sacred things like tobacco. When he would put me on his lap and I snuggled into his chest, I could smell the leather pouch through his shirt, and it always provided comfort. This leather seemed a little different. It was more supple. Carefully, I unzipped the wallet. So many places to put cards, money, and change. It was beautiful.

"Wow, this is very generous. Why would he do that?" I asked.

"It's a friendship offering. He wants to become *our* friend. And if something else develops between him and me, then it does. If not, we at least have made a new friend."

"Hmm, that sounds fair," I commented.

"Oh, I guess I should mention that he is the new CEO of Bernardi Fine Leather Goods USA. Have you heard of them?"

"No, I haven't," I lied.

"Neither had I until tonight. I never knew what his dad did, but they moved from Italy to Chicago to set up a US arm of the family business."

"Wow, that is really cool."

"So, why didn't he move back to Chicago?"

"He prefers Denver but goes back often."

"I would like to say thank you. Can I have his number?"

"I'm sure he would appreciate that." Mom forwarded his number, and I texted my gratitude.

CHAPTER 14

Standing in front of the bathroom mirror, I couldn't tell if the dress fit me. All I saw was the plunging neckline exposing "the girls."

"Neepa, come out. Let me see how you look."

"*No way*, Mom! I feel naked in this dress."

"Honey, it's a simple wrap dress. Nothing fancy."

"Well, it doesn't look like it wraps everything," I complained.

"Okay, here, put this on underneath." I cracked the bathroom door, and she handed me a camisole. Slowly, I exited the bathroom.

"Wowzah, Neepa, you look amazing."

"Mom, I don't like it. It feels like it's stuck to my skin. It clings to everything."

"Neepa, honey, the dress fits you perfectly. You have an amazing body. I'm sorry it isn't a pair of jeans and a T-shirt, but you need to look presentable."

"Can I wear a sweater or blazer with it? Please," I begged.

"Okay, okay." Mom went into the wardrobe and took out a black blazer. "Here, try this."

As soon as I slipped it on, my entire body relaxed. Everything was covered. Admiring myself in the mirror, I couldn't help but crack a small smile.

"Now, what are you going to wear on your feet?"

"I have the black flats you got me for Grandma's funeral," I suggested.

"Sure, that should work. Your hair?"

"Braid of course."

"Great, well, you better hurry or you'll miss the bus."

When I finished my hair, Mom came at me with her big fluffy makeup brush. "Mom, stop. That is where I draw the line."

She gave me a pouty look, like I hurt her feelings. "Fine. You're a natural beauty, so you don't need makeup, anyway."

I grabbed my book bag and headed for the door.

"Have a great time, and don't forget to call me when you arrive and again when you leave."

"Okay, will do. Have a great day at work. Love you."

"Love you, too, honey, and I'm so proud of you."

I ran up the driveway to the bus and was the last one to board. Enapay's head was down, looking at his phone, when I kicked his foot to slide over. When he looked up, his jaw dropped.

"Hello!" I said in an eighties-style valley girl accent.

"Who are you?" he asked.

"Hilarious. Enapay, what's wrong with you? Slide over," I demanded.

"Seriously, I didn't recognize you at first. Why so dressed up?"

"I'm going with Leah and her family to the honoring event for her brother."

"Oh, yeah. Well, you look nice."

I blushed, feeling very uncomfortable. "Funny."

"Geez, Neepa, that was a compliment, not a joke!"

I didn't know what to say, so I just punched him in the arm.

"Ouch," he whimpered.

Walking through the halls, it felt like the first day of school all over again. Everyone gawked. I tried to slip into English class without being noticed, but Michael was right there at the door.

"Damn, Chicago, you look good," he announced.

"Ignore him," Ego suggested. *"He is just teasing you."*

One of Michael's friends whispered in his ear as I walked by. Michael shoved him and shouted, "What did you say?"

"Dude, what is wrong with you? I was kidding, sort of."

Michael pushed past him and walked to his seat.

All this attention made me want to hide in the bathroom. Unfortunately, I couldn't do that, so I kept my head down and didn't talk to anyone. Entering the cafeteria was like the parting of the seas. I rushed to our table and buried my face in a book.

"Hey, Neepa," Julie greeted me, placing her tray on the table.

"Hey," I responded in a gloomy voice.

"Wow, Neepa, you look great," Rebecca remarked as she and Enapay arrived.

"Don't say that," Enapay warned. "She may beat you up."

I glared at him.

"Why?" Rebecca asked.

"I hate all this attention. You know me. I like to be in the background."

"Sorry to tell you, but if you keep on looking like that, you will keep on getting attention," Julie stated. "And there is nothing wrong with it. You look beautiful." Julie looked closely at my face. "Damn, you don't even have any makeup on, do you?"

"No, my mom tried, but I fought her off."

Julie made a face that said smart, natural beauty, plus a killer body.

"I give up," She said, rolling her eyes.

"Neepa, you better get used to it. You're pretty, and people are noticing because you aren't hiding behind your normal twelve-year-old boy wardrobe of jeans and T-shirts," Rebecca added.

My stomach tightened. "What do you mean twelve-year-old wardrobe? It's comfortable." Deep down, I didn't want the attention because I swore I wouldn't be like my mother and get pregnant at sixteen. "How can anyone enjoy this type of attention?" I lamented while wrapping the blazer around me tighter.

Finally, I arrived at my safe place: visual arts class. I walked up to Leah.

"Hi, Leah. Ready for tonight?"

"Yeah, I guess so," she mumbled. "I hope I can hold it together."

"You *will* be fine," I assured her. "Remember, what you and your family are doing is helping others. Your brother would be very proud."

Leah smiled. "Thanks. Hey, you look really nice. I love the dress. I tried a wrap dress before, but it didn't look right. Yours looks like they made it specifically for you."

"It's my mom's. To be completely honest, I'm not that comfortable in it, but she said jeans and a T-shirt would not have been appropriate."

When the bell rang, Leah reminded me to meet her out front. Her parents would drive us to the event.

The second half of the day went exactly as the first. Everyone looked at me, and all I wanted to do was hide. When the final bell rang, I ran out of school. Exiting, I noticed a fancy SUV parked right in front. The tinted backseat window rolled down, revealing Leah. She waved at me.

"Come on, Neepa."

I hurried over to the car and got in. Looking around, I knew this was the nicest car I had ever been in. Immediately, Ego jumped in.

"You don't belong with these people. They're rich and are going to look down on you. Don't go! You'll regret it."

Before her dad started to drive, he and Leah's mom looked back to introduce themselves. "Neepa, we wish the first time meeting you was under different circumstances, but we're so glad you could join us this evening," her mom said. "Leah has told us so much about you and how you have helped her through this difficult time."

"It's nice to meet you both, and I'm truly sorry for your loss." Leah could tell I was nervous. She put her hand on my arm and gave it a quick squeeze.

"The event starts at six o'clock, but we could hit traffic, so just settle in and relax," her dad remarked.

"So, Leah, what actually is going to happen tonight?" I asked quietly.

"It's a theatrical production, where the actors perform various forms of bullying and what people can do to stop, help, and support others. Our fund is the principal supporter of the event, as well as the school crisis hotline. There will be a brief ceremony at the beginning. The president of the college will announce the John Michaels Anti-Bullying Support Fund."

"Seriously? This is so much bigger than I thought it would be."

"Well, when you give a million dollars, the school makes a big deal out of it," her dad replied.

I looked at Leah and mouthed, *One million dollars!* She giggled and nodded her head.

We pulled up to the front of an extensive stone building with massive arches.

Confused, I asked, "Is this a church?"

"No, this is the college theater arts building," Leah's mom replied.

A man greeted us and opened all the car doors to help us exit the car. Once we were out, he got in and drove away. I looked at Leah with concern, and she whispered, "Valet parking." This was all so new to me, and Ego was relentless.

"Your dress is too tight; they will think poorly of you. You don't know what you are doing, and you don't belong with these people."

"Ego, piss off!" I said under my breath. This was not about me. I was here to support a friend, a real friend, and nothing was going to stop me from doing it.

Students and alumni, news reporters and cameras, college staff and board members filled the reception area. I quickly grabbed my phone and texted Mom that we had arrived, sending her a head-blown emoji. The president of the college greeted us and introduced Leah's parents to the college board and other VIPs. We hung back and took it all in. A reporter approached Leah's mom and dad to interview them about the intent of the fund. She then turned to Leah and me.

"So, ladies, what are your feelings about all of this?" The camera swung from the Michaels to Leah and me.

"I think this is very important. I don't want what happened to my brother to happen to anyone else."

"Thank you. And you, what are your thoughts?"

I could feel my body temperature rise and everyone staring at me. Then I heard, *"Butterfly, you got this."*

"What the Michaels family is doing is extremely valuable. My entire life, I have been bullied. Most people only see the physical part, but what is worse is the mental. You lose your self-worth, you want to be invisible, and you feel alone. You question whether it's your fault, like you deserve this type of treatment. If not managed, you create your own bully inside. No one else needs to say anything because you do it all on your own. Only until I realized it was not my fault and the person who is doing the bullying has issues that haven't been dealt with, did I find the courage to stand up for myself. Providing this type of education and support network can make an enormous difference in the lives of so many." It seemed like the world had stopped. I scanned the room, and in return, all I saw were eyes looking at me.

"Thank you. That was amazing," the reporter commented. "And your name is?"

Leah hit my arm, as I didn't realize she was still speaking to me. "Oh, Neepa Irving."

"Neepa, thank you for your honesty."

Leah turned to me. "Holy shit, Neepa, I can't believe you said that."

"Was it wrong?"

"No, it was perfect," Leah's mom responded. "Seems like you knew just what needed to be said."

When we sat in our seats, I texted Mom again.

Crazy night. So much to tell you. I might be on the news.

As predicted, I made the nine o'clock news. When I walked into the apartment, Mom greeted me with a gigantic hug.

"I didn't think you could make me prouder, but you did it again. What you said was amazing."

"Really? I just told the truth."

"I know. That is why it was so impactful. You had the courage to speak your truth. Most people aren't that brave. Mom took my hand and dragged me to the couch. Her excitement was palpable. "So, tell me everything."

Mom hung on my every word. It almost felt like we were becoming best friends. That evening, I dreamt of a butterfly emerging from its chrysalis.

BUTTERFLY

*Adult butterflies break away from their chrysalis
to soar through the air on newly formed wings.*

CHAPTER 15

Winter break and the holidays were just around the corner, and Mom had to work, so I needed to keep myself occupied. This was not unusual, but at least when we lived in Chicago, I had Grandpa or Grandma to keep me company. Enapay and Josie were going back to North Dakota to visit family, so I was completely on my own.

After biology, I heard my name called over the intercom, stating that I needed to go down to the administration office. In unison, everyone in the hall said, "Ooh, you're in trouble." *Sometimes* I felt like I was still in middle school. As always, Rachel was at the front desk.

"Hey, Neepa. How have you been?"

"Good."

"Saw you on the news the other night. You really made an impression."

"Thank you," I replied shyly.

"Principal Fern is ready to see you."

"Oh, okay. Thanks." Not having a clue what was going on, I got nervous.

"You must have done something wrong," Ego predicted.

I knocked on his door.

"Come on in."

I cracked it open and poked my head in. "Mr. Fern, you wanted to see me?" My nervousness was apparent.

"Yes, Neepa, come on in, and no, you're not in trouble." My body relaxed, and I gave a sigh of relief. "First, I wanted to say thank you for the autographed Cubs program. That was very thoughtful of you."

"Well, it meant a lot to my grandpa, and I knew you would appreciate it, so I wanted you to have it."

"That means a lot to me. Now, the reason I asked you to see me today was to speak to you about a program that the superintendent of schools has asked me to spearhead. She would like to create a program to roll out district wide to reduce bullying in our schools and enhance our current support and crisis program. The superintendent asked specifically for you to be involved."

"Me? Why?"

"She, along with many other people, saw your interview the other night on the news. You have firsthand experience and were able to successfully manage a tough situation with grace and understanding."

"Wow, okay. What do I need to do?" I asked with trepidation.

"I'm looking for a small team of students who can work with the faculty and me to develop a blueprint or strategy for this program, and I would like you to assemble that team. Off the top of your head, can you think of at least a couple of other students who might be a good fit for this project?"

Thinking about his request, I realized I knew a couple of people who would be perfect.

"Yes, but there is no guarantee they'll say yes."

"Do what you can. So, I'll take your response as a yes that you will help spearhead the student portion with me?"

I paused for a moment.

"Are you sure you can do this?" Ego questioned. *"You're going to have to relive the past."*

"Sure," I answered.

"Wonderful. Think about it over break, and I'll set a meeting for us in the New Year. Make sure you see Rachel to get a pass," he directed. "Thank you, Neepa, you're going to make such a difference in so many lives."

Waiting for Rachel to complete my late pass, I stared into the depths of the pea-green-painted wall. "Neepa. Earth to Neepa. Here is your pass, and congratulations. I knew you were a different kind of kid."

Rushing down the hall to get to visual arts class, I tried to sneak in without interrupting. Instead, I kicked a chair, which caused me to trip and fall onto an unsuspecting classmate. Once I composed myself, I dropped the late pass on Mr. Taylor's desk and headed for my seat. He stopped speaking and looked right at me.

"Glad you could join us, Neepa, and thank you for the words of wisdom you shared with the world the other night."

My cheeks blushed, and my heart pounded so loud I could hear it in my head. Sheepishly, I acknowledged his comment and sat down.

When the bell rang, a few kids who I had never spoken to before walked past and said, "It's nice to finally be heard."

Leah smiled as I approached her. "Nice job. Seems like you hit a nerve."

"I guess there are more kids out there like me than I thought. Honestly, I thought it was only my problem."

"Isn't that the real problem? Kids feeling like they're all alone?"

"Exactly. Hey, I wanted to ask you something. Would you like to work on a project with me?"

"For visual arts?"

"No, Mr. Fern has asked me to work with him to create a program for the district around anti-bullying and crisis support."

"Seriously?" she screamed.

"Yeah, kind of crazy, isn't it? He told me that the superintendent asked specifically for me to be a part of the planning. He wants me to create a small group to work with him and the teachers to build the student program. So, are you game?"

"Definitely."

"Who else are you going to ask?"

"There is one other person, but I don't want to say anything until he agrees."

"He?"

"Yup."

"Cool." Right before we parted to go to our next class, Leah asked, "What are you doing for the holidays?"

"Nothing, staying here. My mom has to work. And we have my grandparents' house to deal with. But since it's just us, it'll be a quiet break."

"Well, we're going skiing. Mom wants to keep us active since it will be our first Christmas without John. You are more than welcome to join us for a weekend of skiing. We have a house in the mountains, so we have plenty of room."

"Thanks, but I don't know how to ski, and I don't have equipment either."

"Don't worry about that. I can teach you. Plus, we have enough stuff to outfit an entire ski team. I'm sure we can find what you need."

"Everything?"

Leah laughed. "Sure, we've got everything."

"I'll let you know tomorrow once I talk with my mom."

"Okay, that sounds really cool. I hope you'll be able to come."

The following day at lunch, I excused myself from my friends and headed to the popular side of the cafeteria in search of Michael. He wasn't hard to find since all the athletes sat in the same area. I had never been to that side of the lunchroom before, so I was a bit intimidated. Walking in his direction, one of his friends noticed me and nudged Michael.

He looked over. "Chicago, what's up?"

"Hey, Michael, can I speak with you?"

"Sure."

"In private?" I asked quietly.

The table broke out in whispers. Michael looked at all of them and said, "Really?" We walked over to an empty table, and I gave him a recap of the project with Mr. Fern.

"That's great, Chicago, but what does that have to do with me?"

"Well, I wanted to know if you would join the working team."

"Me? Why would you ask me? I have never been bullied."

My face said otherwise, and then he realized what I was referring to. He looked around to make sure no one was listening.

"Oh no, Chicago. Not me."

"Michael, do you know how much influence you have? Popular guy, good-looking, football player, top of the class. People pay attention to you, and if you condemn bullying, people will listen."

"I'm sorry, did I hear you say good-looking?"

I blushed.

His face turned serious. "Neepa, I don't want people to know about . . ."

"Don't worry, you don't have to say anything, but you know what it's like to feel alone. That's the type of experience we need."

"I don't know." He looked at me, shaking his head.

"Would you just think about it, and you can tell me after break?"

"Hey, Michael. Come on, let's go," one of his friends yelled out.

"Fine, I'll let you know after break."

"Thanks."

That evening when Mom returned from work, she wasn't her normal energetic self.

"Hi, Mom, what's the matter? You look down."

"Hi, honey. I just heard from the real estate agent that the water heater at Grandma and Grandpa's house broke down. It has to be replaced before we can put it on the market. I'm going to need to use what is left of our savings to get a new one. Christmas, unfortunately, will be tight."

"Don't worry, Mom, we have each other, and that is all that matters."

"Thank you, honey. I had hopes of making this holiday really special."

"Please, Mom, don't worry about it," I reassured her.

She came over and hugged me. "So, how was your day?"

"Pretty amazing. I didn't mention this to you yesterday because I was still figuring things out, but Mr. Fern asked me to work with him to spearhead a district-wide anti-bullying strategy and to enhance the crisis helpline. The superintendent of schools asked specifically that I help on this project."

"Oh, Neepa. That is wonderful," Mom gushed. "This all came from your interview the other night, didn't it?"

"That's what he said, plus how I handled the T situation."

"Honey, you're growing into such a strong young woman."

"Thanks. Oh, and Leah asked if I could go skiing with her family for a weekend over the break," I said excitedly.

"I don't know. You don't have any equipment. We would have to purchase a lift ticket, and how would you get there? I have to work."

"Leah said they have a house up there and enough equipment to outfit a ski team."

"That is very nice of them, but again, you still need a lift ticket and transportation since you wouldn't be spending the full break with them. Plus, I need you around here. Especially now that I have more to take care of before we can put Grandma's house up for sale." Mom could see the disappointment growing on my face.

"Okay, I'll let her know I can't go."

"I'm sorry, Neepa. I didn't expect the water heater to go out."

"I know, Mom. I understand."

On the last day of school before break, everyone was already checked out. The semester was done, exams were over, and it was just a formality to hold classes. Everyone was talking about what they were doing for break, and it seemed like just about everyone was taking a trip. I avoided the discussion.

When I walked into visual arts class, Mr. Taylor handed me a package wrapped in brown paper. "Neepa, I just finished this last night. I hope your mom likes it. You did some amazing work."

"Thank you. I'm so excited to see it." I took the package and carefully unwrapped it. A lavender-colored paper with white, green, and gold flecks covered the book. The inside page said:

Nature's Wisdom

Poems by Alfred Irving

Illustrations by Alfred and Neepa Irving.

Seeing my name as the illustrator of a book was extremely emotional for me. Even though I knew my grandparents were aware of everything I did, it would have been nice to show them this in person.

"Neepa, I just loved how you took your grandfather's black-and-white drawings and brought them to life with amazing colors and additional details. It's a work of art that you should be very proud of."

"Thank you, Mr. Taylor. I wouldn't have been able to do this without your help and encouragement."

"My pleasure."

I carefully rewrapped the book and placed it in my book bag.

During lunch, Rachel from the administration office walked over to our table.

"Hey, Rachel."

"Hi, Neepa," she replied, nodding to everyone else at the table.

"Hey, I wanted to give you this." She handed me a neatly wrapped package tied with a red ribbon. "Happy holidays."

"Really? Thank you. You didn't have to do that."

"I know, but I wanted to share a series of books with you that I just finished. I thought you would find them interesting. Admittedly, I dog-eared several pages throughout because they had such important reminders. I hope you enjoy reading them as much as I did. When you are done, please pass them on to someone else who might also benefit from the stories."

"Rachel, that's so kind of you. Thank you."

Before she left, Michael caught sight of her from the other side of the cafeteria. He stood on a chair and serenaded her.

"Oh, Rachel from administration. Your hall passes and detention notices fill me with . . ."

"Oh, shoot. Michael just loves to embarrass me. I gotta go." Rachel lowered her head and rushed out of the room.

As soon as she escaped, that side of the cafeteria erupted in laughter.

"That's enough, Michael," the lunchroom monitor announced.

"Are you going to open it up?" Rebecca asked.

I thought about it for a moment. "No, I'm going to wait 'til Christmas."

The bell rang, and we all headed our separate ways. Before Leah and I parted, I let her know I wouldn't be able to join her skiing.

"Can I ask why?"

"My mom has to work, and she needs me around to help with my grandma's house issues by phone."

"Oh," Leah said with disappointment in her eyes. "I understand. Maybe another time."

Since it was just Mom and me for the holidays and we needed to save money, making the house festive was not a priority. We had many holidays like this before, so it didn't bother me. All that mattered was that Mom and I were together. However, just before Josie and Enapay left, I borrowed a couple of strings of lights and hung them around the door and window. To finish my Christmas decorating, I tied the gold ribbon from Marco's gift to me around Mom's gift and hid it under the bed. At least we'd have a little holiday cheer.

As I prepared dinner, I received a text from Marco. *That's weird. I wonder why he's texting me.*

"Is your mom home yet?"

"Not yet, but soon. Why?"

"Can I stop by? I have a surprise for her."

"Sure."

Fifteen minutes later, I heard a knock on the door. When I opened it, I came face to branch with a gorgeous Christmas tree that filled the doorway.

"Can you help me with this?" Marco grunted.

"Ah, sure."

Once in the house, Marco asked me to hold the tree so he could go back to his car to get the stand and two additional bags.

"What is this all about?" I asked.

"Your mom was sharing with me how she wanted to make this a special Christmas for you and her, but the hot water heater ruined her plans. So, I thought I would help. Let's get this tree in the stand before she comes home."

I was stunned and didn't really know what to do. Marco gave me a look.

"Neepa, are you okay?"

"I think so. No one has ever done something like this for us before."

"Isn't that what friends do?" he asked.

"Yes, I guess so."

Once we set up the tree, I went back to cooking dinner. "Do you want to join us? There's enough."

"No, no. I only wanted to drop this off. Have a great night and happy holidays."

"Yeah, happy holidays."

Once Marco left, I filled the base of the tree with water. It smelled fresh, like my tree in the park. Back in Chicago, Grandma and Grandpa had an artificial tree. This was my first live Christmas tree.

"What on earth?" Mom shrieked as she walked in the door. "Neepa, where did you get this tree from?"

I gingerly crawled out from under the tree, trying to avoid getting scratched by the needles.

"It wasn't me. Marco just dropped it off."

"What?" Her tone softened. "No way. I was telling him the other night about how disappointed I was that I couldn't do something special for you this Christmas. How long ago did he leave?"

"Maybe ten minutes ago. I asked if he wanted to stay for dinner, but he declined. He also brought us decorations."

"How sweet. I noticed the lights around the door and window."

"Oh, I did that," I admitted with a cheesy smile. "Josie let me borrow some lights.

"Honey, thank you."

"Well, you've been working so hard, I wanted to make the house a little festive."

"Neepa, you make every day special." She hugged and gave me a kiss on the cheek. "Well, after dinner, I guess we have a tree to decorate."

After we cleaned up from dinner, Mom put some holiday music on her phone and placed it in a tall glass to amplify the sound. Then we began the festivities. Marco supplied us with everything, from tree lights to colorful bulbs to the perfect glass mosaic star that looked like a disco ball when the tree lights were lit. It took up half the apartment, but it was a fantastic tree. We took a selfie in front of it all decorated, and Mom sent it to Marco. He loved the picture and wished Mom and me a wonderful holiday. He would be in Chicago but asked Mom out for New Year's. She gushed.

"Honey, would you be alright if I spent New Year's with Marco?"

"Of course, I'm okay with that."

"But what will you do? Enapay and Josie won't be back by then. Will you be okay by yourself?"

"Sure. Do you remember the friendly woman who works in the administration office at school?"

"Yes."

"Well, she gave me some books for a holiday gift, so I'll have plenty to do."

On Christmas morning, the yummy smells of chocolate chip pancakes and sausage woke me from a sound sleep. I slipped out of bed, snuck up behind Mom, and gave her a bear hug.

"Merry Christmas, Mom."

"Oh, Merry Christmas, honey. Are you ready for breakfast?"

"Definitely. Everything smells fantastic."

"You sound surprised. You know I can cook when I really want to."

"Oh, so all this time, you didn't really want to?"

Mom quickly turned away so as not to get caught in her own exaggeration. The table was set with freshly squeezed orange juice and real maple syrup. Mom set down two plates stacked high with pancakes and a half dozen sausage links each.

"Whoa, Mom. I guess you're hungry?"

"What better way to start a wonderful day than having a leisurely, fattening breakfast with my daughter?"

The pancakes were delicious, and yes, I ate everything on my plate. Afterward, Mom and I slumped down into the kitchen chairs to let our food digest. Mom sipped her coffee, and I rubbed my belly. It had been a long time since we were both so relaxed and comfortable.

"Mom, let's go over to the couch."

"Oh, honey, I can't move."

I walked over, gently stepped on her feet so I could pull her up, and brought her over to the couch. The tree looked wonderful, with the lights twinkling and the disco star shining. I ran my fingers over a branch, releasing its pine perfume. I put my fingers to my nose and inhaled deeply. It smelled so good. Before Mom could complain that I made her move, I handed her my gift.

"Neepa, what is this?"

"Merry Christmas, Mom. I hope you like it."

"You shouldn't have."

Slowly, Mom pulled at the ribbon, untying the bow. She carefully opened the paper wrapping and read the title. Her eyes filled with tears. Gently, she turned the pages. "Oh, Neepa, this drawing is fantastic. She cleared her voice and read out loud:

Universe, universe, your depths are vast.

Holding the secrets of the future, present, and past.

Your energy is found in everything that exists.

Help me remember how to live this life in bliss.

When she was done, she closed the book and wrapped her arms around me. "Honey, this is amazing. I didn't know you had such artistic ability."

"I took what Grandpa gave me and enhanced it."

"Did you bind the book as well?"

"No, my visual arts teacher helped me with that part."

"Neepa, you surprise me with something new about you every day. This is an amazing gift."

"Well, Grandpa's poems have helped me. I figured they would help you as well."

Mom then stood up from the couch and went into the wardrobe. She returned with a small box in her hand.

"Neepa, when I gave birth to you, your grandparents gave me this." She handed me the box. Inside was a gold necklace with a heart pendant that had two small diamonds. Mom took the necklace and put it around my neck.

"The diamonds represent stars. You and I were Grandma and Grandpa's stars. They always knew we would do amazing things. I kind of went off track, and slowly, I'm finding my way. But they never lost faith in us."

I ran into the bathroom to look in the mirror. Mom watched as I admired myself. The diamonds were small, but they sparkled like genuine stars in the night.

"Thank you, Mom. This is the best gift ever."

CHAPTER 16

Mom looked gorgeous. It wasn't the outfit; it was the energy that was radiating from her. She was nervous and excited to see Marco, but suddenly I sensed her hesitation.

"Mom, please don't worry about me. I'll be fine."

"But Neepa, what will you do?"

"I told you I have a brilliant series of books that I'm reading, plus I need to work on the anti-bullying crisis plan for Mr. Fern."

"Okay, but please call if you need anything. I'll have my phone near me the entire time."

"Uh-huh."

"Neepa, promise me you'll call if you need anything."

"I promise."

We both jumped when there was a knock on the door. Mom huffed. "Ugh, electric cars. You can't hear them pull up."

She pushed me to answer the door so she could look in the mirror one last time.

"Hi, Marco," I greeted.

"Neepa, Happy New Year!" He handed me two grocery bags.

"What's this?"

"Since you are flying solo this New Year's, I wanted to make sure you had everything that you . . ." his voice trailed off. I turned around and saw Mom walk out of the bathroom.

"Happy New Year," Mom said in an alluring voice.

"Whoa, Mina." To remind them I was still in the room, I cleared my throat. Marco quickly pulled himself together. "Happy New Year. You look amazing."

"Thank you. What did you bring?"

"I wanted to make sure Neepa had everything she needed tonight."

"Is that Chinese food?"

"Yup, hope you like it. It's from my favorite spot. There is also some sparkling cider, ice cream, double chocolate brownies, and caramel popcorn."

"Marco, that is so sweet of you to think of Neepa. Thank you."

"Yes, thank you," I reiterated.

Marco helped Mom put on her coat, and I could see her melt a little. Before they walked out the door, I had already opened all the food containers and was making my first plate.

"Happy New Year, honey."

"Happy New Year," I replied, my mouth full of food. "Have a great time."

After eating most of the Chinese food, I plopped myself on the couch with a tall glass of sparkling cider, a brownie sundae with vanilla ice cream, a sprinkle of caramel corn on top, and settled into my book.

Rachel was spot on when she said I would enjoy these books. Granted, the main character, Evie Prince, was older than me, but the feelings that made her question her life, like fear and not being good enough, and ultimately finding what made her happy resonated with me. Thinking about all the secrets and doubts that Evie had to overcome made me think of my situation. How was I supposed to help others who are being bullied when I couldn't stop it from happening to myself? Doubt crept into my head. I am just a kid who got lucky with one bully. That doesn't mean I have the answers and can help others. Emotion grew within me. I didn't know where it was coming from. I felt uncomfortable, filled with confusion, anger, frustration, and fear.

"I told you it would be hard to relive your bullying experiences," Ego was quick to comment.

The memories were painful to remember. Some were so raw that it felt like it was happening all over again. "Weak," was all I could hear in my head. The sting when T first said that to me was just as strong. Why? Why did T see weakness? Why did kids bully me at the other schools? There must have been something in me that gave them permission to do so. Realizing that rocked my world. There was something about me that said weak.

Being a mixed-race kid on the reservations where we lived wasn't easy. When I was young, it wasn't as bad, but when I got older, my classmates and neighborhood kids were horrible, repeating what their parents would say. I was told I wasn't Native enough, that I didn't look Native or for kids to stay away from me because my mom would take their daddy away. In the inner cities, I saw crime and drugs. Then, on the reservations, I saw hopelessness, alcoholism, and more bullying.

Every time I got bullied, they would say, "If you tell, I'll hit you harder next time." Ultimately, when I was twelve, my mom's "friend" sexually attacked me. To get away, I kicked him in the groin. He said that if I told anyone, he would deny it and tell everyone that I came on to him, and people would believe it because that was how my mother was. Just thinking about those experiences made my heart race and my palms sweat. My mind was in a downward spiral, and Ego was right there to push the toilet handle, sending me down further into the septic system of my mind.

The more I thought about being weak, the more I feared it was true. Was I weak? I never stood up for myself or my mother. That guy tried to take advantage of me and told lies about my mother, but I didn't tell anyone. Was it because I was scared or weak? Is there a difference? Is that why I had always been bullied? Did I bring it on myself?

My stomach ached, and I felt nauseous. Fear paralyzed my body. It was like I was a little kid again, alone, hiding under the table in our apartment. Covering my ears to block out the yelling and violence outside. I could feel the terror all over again when the kids encircled me on the playground, taunting me as they pushed me down and kicked my books.

Curled up into the fetal position, I rocked, trying to soothe my stomach's pain, and cried. I cried harder than I have ever cried before. Harder than when we lost Grandma or Grandpa. Years and years of fear, pain, and anger were gushing out of me. The emotion was like a tsunami, building and building, until it crashed to shore and leveled everything in sight. With the release of the emotion, there was a subsequent release from my stomach, and I barely made it to the bathroom in time.

After I cleaned myself up, I fell right to sleep.

"Butterfly, wake up."

I opened my eyes, and I was in the park under my tree, but there was nothing else around. It was all gray. Grandma and Grandpa were standing in front of me. I tried to go to them, but there was something, an energy, that was keeping us apart. I cried, "Grandma, Grandpa, what is happening?"

"Neepa, calm down. You are okay. What you are feeling and seeing is fear," Grandpa explained.

"Butterfly, you need to release that fear so you can fly," Grandma added.

"I'm scared."

"Butterfly, what scares you?"

"What if it happens again? What if I continue to be bullied or Mom loses her job again? We don't have you and Grandpa. We might have to go back to living that way again."

"Neepa, breathe, honey. Breathe. The more you fear the what-ifs, the larger they grow until you become paralyzed and can't move forward. Release your fear."

"But how?" I cried.

"Connect to the fear of your past—when you were a child. It sits with your younger self. Go as far back as you can remember. That is where the fear lives. Little Neepa wasn't able to let it go. She didn't know how. But you are older now, and you can comfort your younger self. Tell her she is okay and that she is protected. When you give the love and guidance your younger self needs, she will grow more confident and be able to release the fears. You can do this, Neepa." Then Grandpa recited:

Fear, fear, you were once just a seed in my mind.

Yet, you grow and fester over time.

Becoming larger and uglier the longer I keep you in the dark.

Exposing you to the light, I release your hold on my heart.

I jumped when I felt Mom kissing me on my forehead.

"Happy New Year, Neepa." Mom immediately saw the tears in my eyes. "Honey, are you okay? What happened? Did you have a nightmare?"

I sat up and grabbed Mom and hugged her tight.

"Neepa, you're scaring me. Are you okay?"

Once I pulled myself together, I told her about my dream and my fears. How it was scary to be young and left by myself. The noises and everything I heard outside our door. I could feel people's pain. The sadness and hopelessness on the reservations. And kids taking their own lives. Then I told her about the attack and what he said about her.

"Oh, Neepa honey. I'm so sorry. I had no idea. I didn't realize how my actions were impacting you." She held my face in her hands and looked me square in the face. "One thing I want to make clear is it was not your fault he attacked you. He was and still is a slimeball, and if I ever get the chance to see him again, I'll make sure he doesn't do that to another girl again.

She hugged me tightly. There was a part of me that wanted to break free from her embrace because I was mad at her. There were so many times I needed her when I was younger, and she wasn't there. But I also knew she was just a child herself trying to survive. Slowly, I allowed my body to relax. Mom stroked my hair until I fell back to sleep.

On New Year's Day, I slept until almost noon.

"She's alive," Mom teased me.

"What time is it?" I groaned. My mouth was dry, and my stomach was gurgling.

"Just about noon."

"*Noon!* I slept that long?"

"Yes, but you obviously needed it. What you shared with me last night was a lot, especially all the memories you kept to yourself. I'm so sorry, Neepa, that I wasn't there for you." She paused for a moment, before changing the subject. "There is some leftover Chinese food. Do you want that for lunch?"

"No, I'm good," I said, rubbing my stomach.

Mom came over and crawled into bed with me. "Honey, you scared me last night. Did something happen besides your dream?"

I told her what I had been feeling and that I was afraid I couldn't create an anti-bullying program.

"Why can't you?"

"Because I don't have the answers. I got lucky this last time with T. But there is no guarantee that I won't get bullied again in the future or understand why the person is bullying me. Look at what happened to Leah's brother, and he was in college."

"Neepa, it's okay to be scared. Change and the unknown can be scary. Don't you think it scared me when we moved from Chicago to Denver, or when I lost my job, or when I started my new job? I knew I had to make these changes for you and me. If we wanted a better life, I needed to do things differently. Your support and encouragement have always helped me face my fear. I am here for you; Grandma and Grandpa, Josie, Enapay, and Marco are here. Your friends at school are here for you. You have an amazing support system. Use it and know that you are stronger than you think you are." She kissed me on the forehead.

"Come on, get up. We have a tree to take down."

"No, already?"

"Neepa, it's the first of the year, plus it takes up half the apartment."

I would be sad to see the tree go. It provided enormous comfort, just like my tree in the park. "Mom, when we buy a house, can we make sure that it has lots of trees around it?"

I gently stroked a branch of the Christmas tree and realized how attached I had become.

"Sure, honey, sure."

Slowly and carefully, we undressed the tree, placing each ornament back into the box they came from so we could store them for the following year. Each time we pulled off an ornament, a few needles fell, and the room filled with that wonderful festive smell again. I could tell that even Mom was getting a little sad to take down the tree.

"Mom, can I tell you what Grandma and Grandpa said to me last night?"

"Of course."

"Well, they said that I have to release my fear to be able to fly."

"That makes sense."

"When I asked them how I could release the fear, they told me to speak to my younger self." Mom stopped what she was doing and listened intently. "They said the fear began when I was really young, and if I spoke with my younger self and told her that everything would be okay and that she was protected, the fear would release." I looked at Mom, and her gaze was distant. "Mom, did you hear me? Should I do it?"

"What honey? Oh, sorry, what did you say?"

"Should I do it?"

"Have your grandparents ever steered you wrong?"

"No."

"Well, then you should do it."

We packed up the decorations in silence, and then I asked, "Mom, if you could talk to your younger self, what would you tell her?"

She laughed. "Honey, there are a lot of things I would tell her."

"Seriously, Mom, what is the most important thing that you would tell her?"

Mom let out a tremendous sigh. "I would tell her that just because her life did not look like other people's doesn't mean it wasn't a good life. That my pregnancy was a gift, and even though I didn't get to do teenage kid things, I experienced so much more, and it made me the woman I am today."

"So, you don't regret having me at sixteen?"

"Neepa, I still think sixteen is too young, but you were given to me for a reason. Sometimes, I think it was to keep me alive. Life in Chicago was hard, but because I had you and the support of Grandma and Grandpa, I kept my nose clean and stayed out of trouble. There were plenty of kids I knew who did not fare as well, and I could have been one of them. Listen to your grandparents and talk to your younger self. Assure her that whatever happened to frighten her cannot hurt or scare her anymore."

The neighborhood was quiet, and I had the park all to myself. I brought a blanket to sit on since it was cold and still snow on the ground. With every footstep, I could hear the crunching of the frozen snow beneath my feet. It seemed louder than normal since there were no other sounds to drown it out. Under my tree, I felt fully protected. Eyes closed within my head, I called out to my younger self.

"Little Neepa, can you hear me?"

In a tiny voice, I heard, "Yes."

"Can I speak to you?"

"Yes." I could see Little Neepa cowering in the corner of my mind.

"Are you feeling scared?"

"Uh-huh."

"Why? What makes you afraid?"

"The noise. People are yelling and scaring me. I feel lonely. Momma is always at work, leaving me alone. The mean kids hurt and tease me, saying I'm not worth anything and that I'm stupid because I don't talk."

"How can I make you feel safe?"

I visualized Little Neepa sitting next to me under the tree. I wrapped her in the blanket to keep us warm and rocked her. "Little Neepa, do you know that Mom, Grandma, and Grandpa love you, and we will never have to live in those places or have people hurt us again?"

"I don't believe you."

"Little Neepa, I'll make sure it doesn't happen. I'm older now, and I can protect us. I know more. Mom is different from who she was back then and doesn't have to work all the time. She has always loved us, but now she's learning to love herself as well."

"Do *you* love me?"

"That's a funny question," I replied, feeling shaken inside. *I am talking to my younger self, to myself, so why would she/I ask that question?*

"Do you?" Little Neepa asked again.

"You are me; how could I not love you?"

"I don't feel your love. You say mean things about us and believe that we deserved to be bullied."

It took me a few moments to realize what she was saying. Every time Ego rears its ugly head and I feel doubt or fear, she hears it as well. "I guess I say mean things to us. I'm sorry."

"If you don't love yourself, then you don't love me."

"Little Neepa, I want to love you. I want to love me."

"Then be nice to yourself, believe in yourself, believe in me."

"For such a young person, you are very wise."

"If I'm wise, then you must be as well. You need to recognize that in yourself."

"I'm trying and will focus on loving us as well."

When I opened my eyes, I had pulled my legs up to my chest and was hugging and rocking myself back and forth as tears streamed down my face. Then I heard, "Well done, my butterfly. Well done."

CHAPTER 17

There was less than a week before the new semester would begin, so I took the opportunity while Mom was at work to read and do some research for the anti-bullying program. Before Mom headed out for the day, she said she had a surprise and that I needed to be dressed and ready by five-thirty. Remembering my conversation with Little Neepa, I resolved to love myself and made the effort to look really nice. It wasn't a fancy event, so I didn't have to wear a dress, but Mom said I needed to wear a blouse with my jeans.

After a full day of researching, I took a leisurely shower, washed my hair, and plucked my unibrow-in-training. I wore my hair down and let my natural curls take over. I even put on mascara. When I was done, I inspected myself in the mirror, twirling to see how my curls bounced. Not too bad. I went into the wardrobe and scanned through Mom's clothes. The blouse I'd worn before wasn't comfortable, so I tried on another one, this time a light pink top. It wasn't as tight, but it still felt uncomfortable.

At exactly five-thirty, I heard Mom pull into the driveway and honk. Grabbing my coat, I put my special wallet into my pocket and headed out. Mom was all smiles when I got into the car.

"Neepa, I love your hair. Why don't you wear it that way more often?" She then inspected my face. "Are you wearing makeup?"

"Only mascara," I responded defensively.

"Well, honey, you look fantastic. Are you ready for an amazing experience?"

"What do you mean? Where are we going?"

"Well, Marco is having a photoshoot for his new bag line, and he invited us to sit in and watch. After that, we'll grab some dinner."

"Really, that is so cool. So will these pictures be in those fancy clothes magazines?"

"I believe so."

The address Marco gave Mom led us to an old warehouse. It looked a little sketchy. Mom grabbed my hand as we walked. Once inside, we saw lights, makeup, models, and an array of stunning leather bags. We were like kids in a candy store.

"Mina, Neepa, over here," Marco called. Marco greeted us with a kiss on both of our cheeks and introduced us to the photographer. "Ladies, this is Francesco, the best photographer in the world."

"Oh, you are so kind. He obviously wants me to do a good job, so he is buttering me up," Francesco replied in a heavy Italian accent. Francesco took my hand and said, "Bella ragazza," then went to work.

"What did he say?" I asked Marco.

"Oh, he said you are a beautiful girl."

My face flushed.

"Well, it's true," Mom proudly chimed in.

"Yes, it is, and we Italians pride ourselves on recognizing beauty," Marco added.

It was amazing to see how the models made already exquisite bags look even more incredible. When they broke for the evening, I wandered over to the bag table. Gently, I picked up each one, smelled it, and admired its beauty and artistry. To my surprise, Francesco took pictures of me fawning over the bags. Then I heard him say, "Bella, look at me." When I looked up, he took more pictures. "Hold the bag," Francesco instructed. "Beautiful. Now look away." He pointed. "Take that bag; put it on your shoulder. Look down. Great. Now, take this one, put it right next to your face, and look here. Magnifico." Then he walked away.

Mom rushed over. "What just happened?"

"I don't know. I just did what I was told."

Francesco handed Marco the camera to show him the photos from the evening's shoot. Then I heard Marco say, "Yes, yes. Beautiful. I agree. Send those to me so I can review them more this evening."

Marco clapped his hands to end the photoshoot. "Okay, ladies, are we ready for some dinner?" Mom and I both responded with a resounding yes.

"So, what will it be? There is a great Mediterranean restaurant nearby?"

We looked at each other and shrugged our shoulders since we had never eaten Mediterranean food before.

"Trust me, it's good," Marco promised. Even before we entered the restaurant, the delicious aroma of the food wafted through the air.

The host welcomed us and knew Marco by name. "Another photoshoot tonight?" he asked.

"Yes, hopefully, this is the last one. We didn't capture the right look last time, but we had a new model tonight, and I think we got the perfect shots," Marco replied.

A server showed us to our table.

"I have some newbies for you."

"The house specialties?" he asked.

"Please."

Mom glanced over at me with her eyes filled with excitement.

"So, Neepa, what did you think of the photoshoot?" Marco inquired.

"It was fascinating. Your bags are already amazing, but those models made them look even more spectacular."

"Well, we're trying to sell an image of the person who buys Bernardi Fine Leather goods."

"Why didn't you like the last photoshoot?" Mom asked.

"It was too over the top. I used a different photographer, and we weren't on the same page. Our leather goods are simple. It's the quality of leather and craftsmanship that makes them special. I want anyone who knows quality to want to buy our bags. They're not to be put on a shelf and admired. They're to be used and enjoyed."

I pulled my wallet out of my pocket and put it on the table. "Well, I love mine."

Marco beamed, knowing that I enjoyed his gift. "So, Mina, which bag did you like?"

"There was a beautiful square shoulder bag that looked gorgeous."

"Yes, I know the one. That is one of my favorites as well."

"Neepa, I saw you looking at the cross-body bag. Am I right?"

"Yes," I blushed. "That one caught my eye."

Before anything else was said, the server brought over three platters filled with kabobs, salads, saffron rice, and grilled vegetables. The aroma was like nothing I had smelled before.

"Enjoy," the server offered before he left.

Conversation came to a halt as we eagerly filled our plates. After several minutes of utensils clanking, mms, and wows, we finally came up for air. We laughed, realizing how ridiculous we all looked.

"Was I right, or was I right?" Marco playfully asked.

"Marco, this is amazing. I love it all," Mom confessed.

"Good, I love to see you happy," Marco said with a glint in his eyes.

"Neepa, what do you think?"

"This is good," I replied, my mouth full.

"Neepa!" Mom scolded.

We finished the meal with a sampling of Persian ice cream and baklava. Mom picked up her napkin and threw it on the table. "That's it. I am done. Not another bite," she declared. "Marco, thank you for a wonderful evening. We had two firsts in one night: a photoshoot and Mediterranean food. Such a special evening."

"I'm so happy you could join me. You made a work night so much more enjoyable."

We sat in silence as our food digested. Before we left, I asked Marco about his foundation.

"Oh, you know about the Bernardi Foundation?"

"I did a little research."

"Good, well, it's fairly new. It was the first thing I established when I took over the company from my father."

"Wait, what are we talking about?" Mom asked.

"The Bernardi Foundation serves and supports the diversity of Chicago through scholarships, internships, and mentorship for young people wanting to make a difference," I responded.

"Oh yes. That is an amazing gift you are giving back to the community."

"Chicago has been good to my family, and the diversity of Chicago is something that needs to be celebrated. There are so many young people doing amazing things. All they need is a little help."

"I know. We have one with us tonight. Neepa made honor roll and was asked to help create a district-wide anti-bullying program," Mom said proudly. "Neepa, we should mention the foundation to the Indian Center."

"Congratulations, Neepa." Marco reached over and fist-bumped me. "Yes, you can tell the Indian Center that they will find all the information on our website. I have an amazing team of young people who run the foundation for me. Neepa, something to think about for the future."

Marco brought us back to our car, and I gave Mom and him a few minutes to say their goodbyes.

Marco opened Mom's door, kissed her on both cheeks and helped her into the car.

"See you later, Neepa."

"Bye, Marco, and thanks for everything."

On the drive home, Mom was chattering away about the evening. "Honey, did you have fun?"

"Totally. So, are you guys a couple?" I asked.

"I'm not sure."

"What do you mean, you're not sure? He is totally head over heels for you, Mom. Do you like him?"

A sweet smile appeared on her face. "Yes, I really do. But do you like him?" she asked, now more concerned with my opinion.

"Yeah, he is a nice guy and treats you really well."

When we arrived home, I felt like the character Bruce Banner turning into the Hulk. I couldn't get out of my shirt fast enough before I ripped it off. I had eaten so much food that the buttons were about to pop open. Slipping into one of my favorite sleep shirts, Mom asked, "Neepa, what did you think of those models?"

"What do you mean?"

"Would you ever do that?"

"Ha!" I busted out laughing. "Are you kidding me? I could never do that." I walked into the bathroom and soaped up my face.

"Why, you *are* beautiful."

After my third splash of water, I grabbed my towel to dry off.

"Ah, Neepa, look at the mess. I swear, you are like a bird in a birdbath when you wash your face."

I took my towel and dried off the counter and mirror. "Mom, *really*. They're tall, skinny, and wear a ton of makeup. That's not me."

"But it could be fun to do it once."

"Sure, once."

"What if I were to tell you that Marco would like to use a few of the photos that Francesco took of you tonight in his campaign?"

"What? Are you serious?"

"Yes, he is, and he said that he would pay you just like the other models."

I stood there in shock. "Why would he want to do that? You already like him."

"Neepa, it's not about me. He said your pictures were natural, and that was exactly what he was looking for."

"Have you seen the pictures?"

"No, he said that he would show them to me once he reviewed them all."

"So this is real?"

"Yes, honey, it is real."

"What do you think?"

"It's up to you, but not everyone gets to be featured in a major magazine."

"Can I think about it tonight?"

"Of course."

Once in bed, Mom quickly fell asleep as she had to work the next day. I, unfortunately, lay in bed, eyes wide open, thinking about what she said.

"Neepa, don't be serious, you can't be a model," Ego exclaimed.

"Why can't I?" I asked.

"Because you don't look like them, plus everyone will see you. That is not what you do."

"What do you mean not *what I do?* Ego, why do you say I can't?"

"Because we don't know what will happen. This is new and different."

"Little Neepa, what do you think?"

"You can do this. You're beautiful, and you don't have to hide anymore. Don't be afraid. I'm here with you."

"Shall we give it a try, Ego?"

"Whatever."

The next morning, Mom was already gone by the time I was awake. After a few deep breaths to gather my courage, I texted her, saying that I was okay with Marco using the photos if we all agreed they were good. She responded with a big red heart.

"Oh, Little Neepa, what have I done?"

"You are allowing yourself to be seen. I'm proud of you."

When Mom returned home, she handed me a large manila envelope.

"Well, open it," she demanded.

My hands were shaky. Slowly, I pulled out three photos. Mom was peering over my shoulder.

"Oh, Neepa. You look gorgeous."

I was in complete disbelief that this was me. It looked like me, but it didn't at the same time.

"Do you like them?" she asked cautiously.

"Mom, do I really look like that?"

"Yes, honey, you do. Unfortunately, we can't see how we truly look because of all the noise in our heads. We may think our nose is too big or our hair is unruly because someone else may have said that or because we look so different from what they normally portray in magazines. I have always said you are a natural beauty."

"Wow. I can't believe I'm about to do this."

"Honey, there is something else in the envelope."

At the bottom of the envelope was a folded piece of paper that contained an invoice and a check. I went wide-eyed, not believing what I was seeing.

"Let me see," Mom whined. "Oh, Neepa, looks like you need to open a bank account, and I know just the person who can help you." She grinned. "So, are you good?"

"Yes, I am good."

"Great, let's call Marco."

"Hello, Mina."

"Hi, Marco, I have you on speaker. Neepa is here with me."

"So, Neepa, how did you like the photos?"

"I can't believe it's me."

"Beautiful, right? Can I use them?"

I hesitated and then said, "Yes, you can use the photos."

"Wonderful, Neepa. Thank you. This campaign will run in a couple months. The advertising agency will send copies of the magazine when it's live. This is going to be great. Oh, I forgot to mention that a courier will drop off a package tonight." At that moment, we heard a knock on the door.

"Marco, I think it's here. Hold on." Mom motioned for me to open the door.

"Hello, packages for Mina and Neepa Irving."

"Yes, that's us," I replied.

The courier checked me out from head to toe and glanced at Mom. "Great, sign here." I signed and took the two large brown boxes.

"What perfect timing," Marco commented. "Please open them."

The boxes were embossed with Bernardi Leather. I handed Mom hers, and I took mine. Mom squealed as she opened hers.

"No way, Marco. It's beautiful. Such a generous gift. You didn't have to do that."

"So, you like it?" Marco asked.

"Of course. It's amazing!" Mom exclaimed.

I was slower with my package. Once the box was open, I inhaled the beautiful fragrance of leather. Carefully, I removed the sticker that held the tissue paper wrapping and peeled it back. Inside was the cross-shoulder bag I had admired. Gasping, I said, "No way. No way. I love it."

"Well, I couldn't let my two best lady friends not have an item from our newest line. Plus, Neepa, now that you are a Bernardi Leather model and this line's face, you will need to represent both."

"Wait. What? What do you mean this line's face?"

"You are the only model in the campaign, so you could say that you are the line's model spokesperson."

Mom almost dropped the phone. She was jumping up and down wildly. "Neepa, this is crazy wonderful. How do you feel?"

Slowly, I sat down on the bed. "I don't know."

Mom was so excited, she didn't notice that my exuberance didn't match hers.

"Okay, Marco. Thank you for everything. I'll speak with you later tonight." After Mom hung up, she realized I was sitting quietly on the bed. Mom approached me cautiously. "Honey, are you okay?"

"Yeah, I think so," I replied, my head down, inspecting my hands.

Mom took my hands in hers. "What's wrong?"

"It just hit me that everyone will see my picture."

"Isn't that good?" The fear in my eyes said differently. "Neepa, do you think you would recognize a model from a magazine?"

I thought about her question for a few moments. "Probably not."

"Exactly. It was an amazing experience. You made some money, and you helped a friend. Don't worry, honey."

I thought about it some more.

"You got this," rang loud and clear in the back of my head. Then I heard Little Neepa's giggle. I exhaled a huge sigh. "If you say so."

"Thanks, Mom."

"My pleasure."

Vacation was over, and the clock alarm sounded like fingernails running down a chalkboard. Six-thirty was way too early to be awake. The lingering smell of Mom's coffee and perfume urged me to get up. Stubbing my toe on the shower stall sent a throbbing pain through my foot, waking me completely. I threw on my normal school uniform of jeans and a T-shirt, pulled back my wet hair, brushed my teeth, and grabbed a bagel and orange for the road. I hadn't seen Enapay for a couple of weeks. As I approached the bus stop, it was silent. No one talked and everyone appeared as lethargic as me, including Enapay.

"Hey," I greeted as I punched him in the shoulder.

"Ouch. Really, that is how you greet me after not seeing me all vacation? Nice to see you too, Neepa."

"When did you guys get back?"

"Late last night," he groaned. "I pretended to be sick this morning, but Mom made me get up."

"Did you have fun?"

"Yeah, it was nice seeing family, but I didn't miss being back on the rez. Half the time, we didn't have cell service or internet, and when we did, it was spotty. I forgot how different life is up there.

"Mom said we had been to your rez, but I don't remember. Is it nice?"

"It's nice if you like wide open spaces and no internet. Every year we go back, there are improvements, but there is still a lot of poverty as well. How was your vacation? Did you do anything fun?"

I smiled. "Not much. Mom had to work, and I helped her figure things out with Grandma's house."

It was the first class of the day, and I was already staring at the school clock. One Mississippi, two Mississippi, three Mississippi. I swore it was running slow. I dug my fingernails into the palm of my other hand to keep me awake.

It even felt like the teachers were speaking slower than normal. It was clear no one had wanted vacation to end. On a positive note, it was nice to see everyone at lunch. It made me realize how special Leah, Enapay, Rebecca, and Julie had become to me. The cafeteria was packed, and the volume level was high. I headed for our regular table. Enapay was in line to buy lunch, and Rebecca and Julie were late to get to the lunchroom. Leah and I were the first ones there.

"Leah, how was skiing?" Her nose and bottom half of her face were a shade darker than the rest, enhancing her raccoon eyes.

"The snow was great, but it was a tough vacation. Mom tried to keep us busy, but skiing was my brother's favorite hobby. There was a lot of emotion. Probably good that you didn't join us." She then smiled. "It doesn't mean that you can't come later in the season, though." Leah looked around to make sure the others weren't coming yet. "Guess what?"

"What?"

"My brother came to me in my dreams."

"Nice. Did he talk to you?"

"No, but he gave me one of his signature cheesy smiles."

"How do you feel?"

"Good. It makes me happy to know that I have him back in my life."

"Leah, he never left."

She smiled. "So, what did you do over vacation?"

"Yeah, Neepa, you never told us what you were doing over vacation," Rebecca chimed in just as she arrived at the table.

"Not much. My mom had to work. I helped her with some stuff, and I did a lot of reading."

"Did you finish the books that Rachel gave you?" Julie asked.

"Yup, they were great. It made me think about how I'm living my life."

"Wow, sounds deep," Julie commented.

"Yeah, they were, but in an entertaining way. It's all about a woman who has a spiritual awakening and the journey she's on to find her true self."

"Okay, that sounds a little woo-woo," Rebecca interjected."

"Actually, she does a good job of letting people know that it's okay to feel, to be scared, angry, happy. Feeling is a part of growing, and most of the time we push away or hide our feelings. If you're interested, I'll share them once my mom reads them." I paused.

"Don't do it, Neepa, you will regret it," Ego warned.

"I did do something amazing if you want to hear about it." Everyone looked up from their food. "But you all have to promise to keep it a secret."

Their eyes lit up; they stopped eating and leaned in. I looked around to make sure no one was listening and lowered my voice. "I was a model for Bernardi Fine Leather Goods."

"What!" Leah screamed.

"Shhh, keep it down. I don't want anyone to know."

"Wait up, who are we talking about?" Enapay asked, his face all twisted and confused.

"Bernardi Leather," Leah exaggerated. "Like, one of the most exquisite leather brands out there. Don't you remember we searched him on the internet?" Most times, Leah never let on how rich her family was, but today, her upper-crust lifestyle was glaringly apparent. "Rebecca and Julie, you know what I'm talking about, right?"

"Yes," Julie replied. "Those bags are the kind you only see in magazines." Rebecca shrugged her shoulders, clearly indicating that she had no clue what we were talking about.

"Neepa, how did that happen?" Enapay asked. "And why didn't you tell me at the bus stop?"

"It's a long story, but my mom's friend invited us to a photoshoot. The photographer took some photos of me, and now I'll be in their latest campaign."

"Holy shit, Neepa. That's amazing. Can we see the pictures?" Rebecca asked.

"The campaign won't be in magazines for a couple months. I can show you then."

"OMG, Neepa! I'm so excited for you," Leah exclaimed.

"It was only a one-time thing."

"Neepa, how are you going to handle the attention? You almost beat me to a pulp the last time I complimented you," Enapay reminded me.

"My gosh, you are such a drama king. I didn't beat you," I stated. "Mom said that no one will recognize me. Plus, I'm sure no one here looks at the magazines he will advertise this in, so I should be safe."

"For your sake and mine, I hope so as well," Enapay said while rubbing his arm.

CHAPTER 18

A few days passed, and we were back to the normal grind. Up early, bus, classes, lunch with friends, classes, bus, home, park on occasion, homework, dinner, bed. Same thing day in and day out. In my daze of boredom, Mr. Fern's voice broke through the mundane. He spotted me in the hall right before I entered calculus.

"Neepa, can I speak to you?"

"Sure."

"Hope you had a nice vacation."

"I did, thank you."

"Well, I wanted to set up a meeting with the peer group you put together so we could start working on the student portion of the anti-bullying strategy."

"Oh, yeah. I have one definite and one maybe. Can I give you the final names tomorrow?"

"Sure, sure." The bell rang. "Hey, you better get to class." He opened the classroom door, and I headed straight to my seat.

The next day, in English, I pulled Michael aside before he headed to his next class.

"Michael."

"Hey, Chicago, what's up?"

"Have you made your decision?"

He gave me a pained look. Lifting one finger to stop him from answering, I launched into my pitch. "Before you say anything, now that you have some free time since football season is over, I just thought you wouldn't mind helping out. Think of your participation as bringing attention to the issue. If a football player and popular kid thinks anti-bullying is important, then others will think so as well. You don't have to be anything other than an influencer."

"You forgot to say good-looking this time." He smiled, then looked at me, dropping his head in defeat, and mumbled, "Who else is in the peer group?"

"Leah Michaels."

"Who?"

"Her brother was the one who died by suicide."

"Oh, yeah." He hesitated. I gave him my best puppy dog eyes. He tried to look away, then said, "Fine. I'll help. Another thing for my college resume. Ivy's want more than just grades."

My excitement got the best of me, and I lunged at Michael and hugged him. Realizing what I had done, I quickly retreated. Michael seemed as stunned as me.

"Um, great. Thanks. Mr. Fern will set the first meeting," I blurted and hurried away.

"Thank you, everyone, for joining me this afternoon. Just so we're all on the same page as to who is helping with this project, let me run through who is in the room. When I mention your affiliation, please raise your hand. We have elementary and middle school district representatives, the deans for each high school grade, school security, our local law enforcement, guidance counselors, and one teacher from each grade. As you know, we are here to discuss the strategy and development of an anti-bullying and crisis support program for the district. To help us is our student peer group: Neepa Irving, Leah Michaels, and Michael Beekman," Mr. Fern announced. "I have asked the student peer group to outline a student program for the high school that can be modified for our middle and elementary schools. The superintendent has asked that we have a plan developed before the end of the school year that will be presented to the superintendent and principals of the district schools. Once it has been agreed to, then it will be proposed to the board of education for approval. We have a lot of work ahead of us, and I want to thank each one of you in advance for your dedication to this important initiative."

I glanced over at Leah and Michael to see if they were as freaked out as I was. Both were sitting stiffly in their seats, not daring to move.

"Neepa, I would like to thank you for your brutal honesty concerning your experience with bullying that created the spark for this initiative. It takes students like you who are willing to be vulnerable to make a difference in the lives of others."

His comment earned a round of applause. I quickly acknowledged the comment and then looked down at my feet. A few other teachers made statements before the meeting concluded.

Leah looked at me. "Holy crap, Neepa, I didn't know this would go to the board of education."

"Neither did I. Mr. Fern conveniently left out that part when he asked me to help."

"How much time is this going to take? He does know we're still students, right?" Michael asked nervously.

"Yes, I *am* aware, and yes, I did leave out a few details when I asked you, Neepa." Mr. Fern's presence startled us.

"Sorry, sir, I didn't know you were there," Michael remarked.

"I know it sounds like a lot, but we really need the day-to-day intelligence that you all have. I'm looking for your insights and understanding of our student body. Teachers and principals don't have our ears to the ground like you all do. Your guidance and feedback are critical to this process. We can build an in-depth plan, but if students don't buy in, then it's worthless. Neepa, can I get some ideas of what you all think a student-focused program should look like by the end of next week?"

I glanced at Leah and Michael. "Ah, yeah. Sure, we can get you something by then."

"Great. I'll have Rachel schedule biweekly planning meetings for us to make sure you have the support you need. Oh, I almost forgot to mention that there will be college recommendations waiting for you at the end of this process. Michael, that should ease some of your concerns as you enter your senior year."

"Yes, sir, it does. Thank you."

Mr. Fern thanked us again before walking away.

"So, can you guys meet tomorrow after school for an hour or more?" I asked.

"Sure, that works for me. Yup, can do. Where?" Michael asked.

We all looked at each other. "We can meet at my house," Leah offered. "My parents won't be home from work until after five o'clock, so that should give us an uninterrupted hour plus."

"Sounds good. Give me your numbers just in case something comes up," Michael requested.

Leah looked at me. "Neepa, I can give you a ride tomorrow."

"Great, thanks."

That evening, I gave Mom the rundown of what the initiative was about. "Neepa, this is much bigger than you let on."

"I didn't know until today that it was going up to the board of education. Oh, and Mr. Fern said that we would all receive college recommendations for our participation."

Mom's breath caught in her throat, making her gasp for air.

"Mom, you, okay?"

She cleared her throat. "Yes, just the thought of you leaving me and going to college caught me off guard."

"Don't worry, Mom, it won't happen for another couple years, and I'm sure Marco has plans for you two besides."

Mom blushed. "Honey, I've never been without you. I'll miss you. But enough of that, we still have time." She quickly tried to change the mood. "So, who else is working with you on this project?"

"Leah and Michael."

"Michael who?"

"His name is Michael Beekman. He's a football player, popular guy, blah, blah, blah."

"How did you get him on this project? Doesn't sound like he would be the type."

"I helped him in a time of need. Plus, he needs the recommendation for college."

"My girl . . . always helping others."

Over dinner, Mom and I discussed my initial thoughts about the anti-bullying program. The dialogue between us made it feel like we were work colleagues. Picking her brain and sharing my research got the wheels turning for the strategy meeting with Leah and Michael. I cleared the table and was putting the leftover pasta in the refrigerator when I heard Mom giggle.

I turned to ask what was so funny. Mom was texting on her phone. Her smile lit up her entire face. *Marco.* She looked up when she finished.

"Mom, we have our first meeting tomorrow after school, over at Leah's house."

"How are you getting there?"

"Leah drives to school, so I'll catch a ride with her."

"And home?"

"I'm sure she can give me a ride home. If not, I'll call you."

She smiled. "Neepa, if I haven't told you lately, I'm really proud of you."

"Thanks, Mom."

Leah's house was in a neighborhood I hadn't been to before. Slowing down, she turned onto a road with a small house in the middle and a gate. As we approached, the gate lifted, and a man waved. I looked at Leah and mouthed, *Who are you?* She laughed. Each house we passed, or should I say each mansion, seemed to get bigger and fancier. Finally, she turned into a circular driveway and pushed the garage door opener. My mouth dropped at the enormity of the house. Windows were everywhere. Leah parked and grabbed her stuff from the back.

"Are you coming?" She looked at me through the seats.

"Ah, yeah."

We entered the house through the garage that led to a mudroom. She turned off the alarm and dropped her bag on the bench.

"You can put your coat and stuff here. I have to tell the guard that Michael is coming over." She walked away from me to make the call. "Hey, you hungry?"

I didn't answer.

"Neepa, are you okay?"

"Sorry, I just haven't been in a house like this before."

"Stop it. Make yourself at home. Are you hungry?"

"Yeah, sure."

Leah went into the pantry and pulled out a few bags of chips and some cookies, then grabbed drinks and grapes from the refrigerator.

"Michael should be here any moment."

Just then, the doorbell rang, and Leah ran to answer it.

"What, no butler?" Michael asked.

"Ha, ha, hilarious."

"No, seriously, this house looks like there should be a butler."

"Come on, we're in the kitchen."

When Michael entered, he looked at me like *WTF*. I put my head down to hide my laugh.

"Help yourself to the food. We have a good hour before my mom will be home, so I suggest we get started, unless you want her telling us what to do." She looked over at me.

"Okay. So, I thought I would start by telling you both why I asked you to join me in the peer group."

"Yeah, that would be nice," Michael stated with a grin on his face.

"Leah, you and your family have already made efforts to make change, and I thought you could bring insight into the crisis support work. Michael, eventually, we'll need to roll out a program at school, and I was hoping your popularity at school would help get more people on board." It seemed that Michael sat up a little straighter after hearing my assessment of him.

I continued, "If a jock thinks this is important, then I'm certain others will too. And finally, me. Well, you both know why I was asked to do this work, but I'm sure we all have had experiences we can draw on to develop this plan." I grabbed a bag of chips and shoved a few in my mouth. "So, over winter break, I was doing some research."

"You worked on this over winter break?" Michael asked incredulously.

I ignored his comment. "The research suggests that a plan like this cannot be centralized in one place. There are many groups that play a role, and all must have a strategy."

"Yeah, but we're only responsible for the student portion, right?" Michael asked.

"Yes, but we have to get students to work with the other groups, like the counselors and law enforcement."

"Law enforcement. Wow, I didn't even think about them. I was only thinking about school security," Leah added.

"Yeah, if things get really bad for someone, they can arrest the bully for assault or something worse." That seemed to have struck a chord in all of us, and we realized the seriousness of what Mr. Fern had asked us to do. The hour flew by, but we established a good rapport and started brainstorming some ideas for the student plan.

"We have less than a couple weeks before we'll meet again with Mr. Fern. How often do we want to connect? Can you guys do three days a week?" I asked.

"Depending on the day, my dad has me doing a few things after school," Michael explained.

"Well, if you can't make it, I can bring you up to speed in English or we can connect at lunch."

"Sounds good. So tomorrow, same time? I should be able to be here."

"Great. And we can meet here again if that works," Leah offered.

"Leah, that would be great."

"Chicago, do you need a ride home?"

"Yeah, please."

Leah walked us out and waved as we drove away.

"Holy crap, can you believe that house?" Michael's arms were flailing around to convey the size. "My dad makes good money, but her house is like twice the size of mine."

"Would you keep both hands on the steering wheel?"

He looked at me with a disgusted look.

"Did you know that she was that rich?"

"I knew they were rich, but not *that* rich."

"Crazy that with all that money, someone could still bully her brother."

The more we worked together, the more each one of us let our guards down. Stories were told, feelings shared, and a few tears were shed by all of us. One afternoon, we were discussing the outline, and Michael was distracted, constantly looking at his phone.

"Are we keeping you from something?" Leah asked.

"Huh, what?" Michael looked at us both with a somewhat embarrassed look. "Sorry, I have to do something for my father when I get home." We tried to continue our discussion, but Michael's phone rang. "Sorry, got to take this." He stood up and hurried into the mudroom.

Unfortunately, for all of us, his father tore into Michael, and his father's voice was so loud we could hear the conversation all the way in the kitchen. When Michael returned, his demeanor was sullen. He didn't look at either one of us.

"Michael, is everything okay? Do you have to go?" Leah asked.

"No. I don't have to help my father anymore," he replied. "Per my father, I'm too irresponsible."

Neither one of us knew how to respond, but I didn't think he was looking for a response. We worked for another ten minutes, then called it a day. The energy in the room had changed, and it was no use trying to force it.

"Chicago, do you need a ride home?"

Leah looked at me. "Don't worry, Michael, I can take her home tonight. I wanted to show her a new dress I got anyways, unless you want to see it as well?"

"Ah, no. That's okay."

We walked him to the door, but before he got into the car, I yelled after him, "Michael, remember, it's not you." He gave a weak smile and drove away.

By the second week, we had some solid ideas that we felt were good enough to share with Mr. Fern. I stopped by the administration office in the morning to tell Rachel so she could pass along the message.

Prior to the bell ringing for lunch, Rachel's voice came over the loudspeaker, asking Leah, Michael, and me to please come down to the administration office. When we walked in, Rachel led us to the conference room. Mr. Fern joined us with a large pepperoni pizza.

"Thought we could discuss your ideas and have lunch together."

The three of us looked like a pack of jackals, watching Mr. Fern place the pizza on the table. It was apparent we were hungry, so he suggested we grab a slice then get into the discussion.

"So, I understand you have something to show me?"

"Yes, we do." I slid a piece of paper over to him. We all watched him as he ate his pizza and read without skipping a beat.

"Hmm, this is really good."

"The pizza or our ideas?" Michael asked.

"Both. I like how you've included all the groups. Having the school administration and the student body representatives working together to ensure that everyone knows the signs of bullying, creating guidelines that are clear to all so everyone knows where students and teachers can turn for help, and creating a system to safely report a situation. This is comprehensive. I really like the idea of providing this information in new incoming and returning student packets, as well as having the information posted around the school. And holding discussions in appropriate classes is a great way to get the information out to the student body."

Mr. Fern paused momentarily before continuing. "Hosting peer-led discussion groups and having our theater group create a performance highlighting different scenarios and what students can do to support others or get help are also fantastic ideas. And tying in what you've suggested with a monthly check-in by the principal, counselors, and school security will keep everyone who needs to be involved up to date on any issues. Also, your recommendations for working with law enforcement if a situation cannot be managed by school officials, the students involved, parents, or guardians . . . you've thought of more than just what happens at school. For this to be as impactful as we hope it will be, everyone must be on the same page. You've captured that need in what you've detailed. Let me bring this back to the teachers to get their feedback. This is great work," he added, with the biggest smile I'd ever seen on our principal's face.

The three of us were on cloud nine as we walked out of the office. With our bellies full and knowing that he liked our ideas, we couldn't help but jump up and down when we were far enough away from the office door.

By the following week, Mr. Fern gave the green light to build out the student portion of the strategy and identify key areas that needed to be considered for school policies, like physical bullying versus cyberbullying; how counselors could support both the victim and the person doing the bullying; what families would need to be aware of; and when it would be time to bring in law enforcement. Now that the student portion was approved, we scaled back to meeting twice a week at Leah's house. Mr. Fern asked me to review the proposals from the other groups to consider if there was anything we needed to add from the students' perspective. Every free minute, I was working on this strategy.

When Mom came home that evening, she found me lying on the couch. "Honey, are you okay? Are you not well?"

"I don't know. I have no energy."

"Do you need to eat?"

"Maybe. I'm tired. Working on the strategy is starting to wear me down."

"Okay, honey. You rest. I'll order a pizza."

Hearing the knock at the door made my mouth water.

"Pizza's here. Please come and eat." Mom had already set the table so all I had to do was get my butt off the couch. "So tell me what is going on with the strategy."

"I think it's going well, but there are so many moving pieces, I don't know if it will really turn out to be a good plan, and I'm worried about it being presented to the board of education."

"Neepa, there still are a few more steps before it gets presented for final approval, and you're not solely responsible for the outcome. You're a piece, an important one, but others have responsibilities too."

"I know, but the superintendent asked me specifically to do this."

Mom stood up and went into the wardrobe. She pulled out the poem book that I had given to her for Christmas. "Neepa, did Grandpa ever read the ant poem to you?"

"No."

"Well, when I was a kid, he'd pretend his fingers were ants, and he'd run them up and down my arms, giving me shivers. Anyway that doesn't matter . . . what's important are his words. Listen."

Ant, ant, community is your goal.

Always working for the good of the whole.

Your patience is something to behold.

Guide me to trust that all will unfold.

"Neepa, you were chosen to do this work because you care for other people and you're smart. The superintendent is no dummy. Everything you're doing will work out perfectly. Be patient."

She then ran her fingers up and down my arm like an ant, giving me the shivers.

CHAPTER 19

The sound of the door opening interrupted my concentration. I glanced up. Mom averted my gaze when she entered.

"You know, you can text me if you're going to be late," I reminded her. "Your plate is in the oven."

"Sorry, honey." I watched her as she put down her bag and washed her hands.

"Where were you tonight?"

"Oh, I was out with my coworkers."

"But tonight is only Wednesday. I thought that was a Thursday night thing."

"Normally it is, but someone had a conflict."

Tension radiated from Mom, and I knew something was up. Turning my focus back to my homework, I let her eat dinner.

"Neepa, this food is wonderful," she complimented in an over-the-top kind of way.

"Uh-huh." I didn't look at her.

"How's the strategy work coming along?"

"Good." I made sure my response expressed annoyance.

"Honey, are you mad at me?"

"Should I be?"

She finally looked me in the eyes. "What does that mean?"

"If I have nothing to be mad at you for, then I guess I'm not mad."

I could feel her gaze. She finished dinner, put her plate in the dishwasher, and went into the bathroom. When she returned, I had finished my work and started putting away my school stuff. Mom paced around the apartment like a caged animal.

"Neepa, I need to tell you something," she said as she continued to pace. I didn't respond.

"Would you please look at me?" Her furrowed brow told me she was serious. I put my book in my bag and glared at her. "Okay, so I wasn't out with coworkers."

I braced myself.

"I was out with my old boss."

My heart sank, and I was afraid to hear anymore. I stood there, motionless, holding my breath.

"He wanted to see how I was doing and invited me out for drinks. He said he was getting a divorce and wanted to know if we could go back to how things were between us."

To hide my disapproval, I resumed putting away my stuff.

"Neepa, could you please stop?"

I stood there, not looking at her, my anger brewing.

"At first, I thought, wow, we really had something. Then I paid attention to how he was acting and what he was saying, and I realized that he just wanted me for a side piece. I told him I wasn't interested."

I let out a huge breath of air. "Phew." After a few deep breaths, I spoke. "Mom, I'm happy that you realized you're more than a pretty object. You deserve more. But why did you go out with him in the first place? Things seemed to be going so well with Marco, and I know he cares deeply for you."

"I know, honey, but Marco is so good. He is a good man . . ."

"And?"

"And. Wonder if he finds out what type of person I've been. I'm sure he'll leave me . . . us. So why even start if I know how it will end? I'm tired of being hurt and thrown away."

"What do you mean, the type of person you've been? Mom, do you really think you were that horrible of a person?"

"Neepa, I've ruined marriages, put me and us in situations that we should never have been in. He's too good for me."

Confusion followed my annoyance. "I know I haven't dated yet, but doesn't it take two? If someone wanted to leave their wife to be with you, isn't it on them? You're not completely innocent, but they had a choice, right?"

Mom looked away from me.

"Right?" I pushed.

"Yes, they had a choice."

"Mom, you're amazing. You deserve the very best, and I believe Marco wants to give that to you. Be honest with him. Let him make his decision."

Mom dropped her head and chuckled. "Seriously, Neepa, who are you?" She stopped laughing and looked at me tenderly. "Thank you."

"For what?"

"For always believing in me, even when I don't believe in myself. I've carried a lot of shame throughout my life, and my self-esteem disappeared. I never thought I'd be a teenage mother. I had dreams that evaporated when I had to drop out of high school. There were times when I was jealous that I didn't get to have all the high school or college experiences others were enjoying, and I acted out, trying to recapture that time in my life again. But, you made me grow up, even when I didn't want to. You've made me a better person, Neepa Irving, and I'm so glad I get to be your mother."

That evening, Grandma and Grandpa came to me. We sat under my tree together. "Why would Mom do that? Be with a man who she knows is wrong, but push away a man who truly loves her?" I asked.

"Neepa, your intuition is strong. You tell us."

"She doesn't think she's worthy of having a good man by her side and a good life, and that's why she's always gone back to men who treat her wrong. With them, she knew what to expect."

"Exactly," Grandma acknowledged. "Neepa, many people fall into that kind of life. Wanting something better but too afraid to allow it because they don't know what will happen. People like to be comfortable even when the situation is not good."

"Butterfly, if you keep an open heart and believe your intuition will grow stronger, you won't need to rely on us."

"What? I jumped up. Grandpa, are you leaving me? Grandma, you said you would always come."

"No, no, we're not leaving you, but we want you to have confidence in yourself and your gifts. Think of the moose and trust yourself. We are always here with you and will always be."

At Leah's house, we were deeply focused until I broke the silence. "I really think we should have a program about self-worth in this plan."

"What do you mean, self-worth?" Leah asked.

"Bullying takes a toll when you hear the criticisms and harsh words enough. When they are backed up by torment and physical assaults, you believe what's being said to you. You feel you deserve that treatment. Kids need to learn that no one else's opinion of them matters. It's what they believe and how they love themselves that truly matters. It's a skill we all need to learn. I know I struggle with it, and I know grown-ups who struggle as well."

Michael was quick to agree.

"If my brother had more self-worth, he may have said something sooner." Leah's eyes misted over.

"If my grandpa were here, he would say your brother needed to hear the wisdom of the moose."

"The moose?" Leah's voice was strained.

"Yes, my grandpa raised me to always listen to nature. He said it's full of wisdom, and he wrote poems about it that he would share when I needed some guidance. Spiritually, the moose symbolizes self-esteem and confidence."

"Why the moose and not the bear or another animal?" Michael questioned.

"Have you ever heard a bull moose bellow during mating season? He doesn't care who's around; he's loud and proud and ready to get busy. He'll fight whoever, and with that rack, he knows he's *the man*."

"Well, when you put it that way, it makes sense," Michael admitted. "I want to be the moose, loud and proud. Do you remember the poem?"

"Only if you're serious. This isn't something to joke about."

"No, I'm dead serious. As you mentioned, we all need to work on our confidence."

Leah gave a sideways look to Michael. "You need self-confidence?"

"Look, just because I always want to be the center of attention doesn't mean that I'm confident." He lowered his head. "Everyone has their issues, and what you see is not always the truth."

Leah could tell there was something really painful behind that statement, and she left it alone. I looked at Michael and recited the poem:

Moose, moose, your bellow is strong.

Sounding your intentions to all that come along.

Your confidence and self-esteem are as apparent as you are tall.

Help me to remember my worth for once and for all.

After two straight months of work, we finally presented the completed plan to Mr. Fern and the teachers for their review and signoff. They held the meeting after school to specifically ask questions about the plan. Everyone received the plan before the meeting, so there would be enough time to have a meaningful discussion. Back in the administration conference room, Leah, Michael, and I sat at the far end of the table. The rest were seated at the other end. Looking from the outside, you would think we were being interrogated. Needless to say, the three of us felt pretty anxious.

"Leah, Neepa, and Michael. First, let me congratulate you on a job well done." Mr. Fern then turned to the others in the room. "I'm so impressed with these three. I've had the opportunity to get their ideas, feedback, and concerns about this process. The thought they've put into this program is commendable." His eyes turned back to the three of us. "There are some points we need clarified, so let's get into it."

Mr. Fern led a line of questioning that ranged from cyber to physical bullying to our emphasis on respect. "I noticed you've woven respect throughout this entire plan, both for the victim and the bully. Can you explain its importance?"

"There are so many reasons why someone would bully. Fear, jealousy, prejudice, control. The list goes on. Why we feel respect is so important is that when we first respect ourselves, we're less likely to tolerate or be impacted by the bullying."

Leah interjected as smoothly as if I passed her the baton. "If we respect each other for our differences and similarities, we'll stand up for each other if someone is being bullied. And if we give respect to the person who is doing the bullying, we're open to understanding why they are engaging in that type of behavior."

"Everyone has a story, and until we hear it, we cannot understand why someone does what they do," Michael added.

"Very nice. Anyone else have questions?"

"Yes, I do. What's the importance of the moose?" Mr. Taylor asked with a tinge of confusion.

"Oh, I got this one," Michael said assertively. Leah and I both laughed at Michael's enthusiasm. "Spiritually, the moose stands for self-esteem and confidence."

"Why the moose?"

"Funny you should ask. Have you ever heard the bellow of a bull moose when it's mating season? He's loud and not afraid to let others know what he's up to. Plus, with that rack, he knows *he* is the man. He is the epitome of self-esteem."

Mr. Taylor cleared his throat. "Okay then. Thank you for that."

It only took a few days to receive approval on the plan. Mr. Fern arranged the meeting with the superintendent and asked if I would deliver the presentation.

"Me, why me? Can't all three of us do it?" I whined.

"No, this is a formal meeting, and we're under time constraints. She prefers one presenter. You know this plan inside and out, and besides me, you are the only other person who has seen all the elements come together. Plus, she personally asked for you to be a part of this process," Mr. Fern explained.

"Fine, I guess, if there are no other options."

"I wouldn't say there were no other options. But you're the perfect option."

CHAPTER 20

"Neepa, are you ready for this?" Mr. Fern asked with a smile. I know the gesture was meant to ease my mind, but it felt contrived, like he was as nervous as I was.

"I don't know." I paced back and forth. "There are so many people in there. Wonder if they don't like the plan? Wonder if I can't answer their questions? What if they laugh at me?" My heart raced, and my breath quickened. The dampness under my arms spread. His eyes followed me as I walked from place to place.

"Neepa, the plan is sound. You guys did a great job bringing in what we needed to understand and focus on in order to support all students. We all signed off on it. Now you get to deliver it to the superintendent."

"Why don't you do it?" I held out the folder that contained the presentation notes. He shook his head.

"Nope, no can do. This has been a student-led endeavor, as it should be. You, Leah, and Michael deserve all the credit."

"Or criticism."

"Just remember, if there is criticism, it's not directed at you. Remember who signed off on this plan. And, along with us, everyone in that room wants to make sure we do right by the students and reduce the number of bullying instances."

I wanted to believe him, but I would be the person everyone looks at if there is criticism. *What if I can't answer their questions, or worse, I forget what to say?*

I continued to pace. To stop me, he took me by the shoulders and looked me straight in the eyes.

"Neepa, you can do this. I believe in you, but it doesn't matter, if you don't believe in yourself."

I nodded.

"You were made to do this, and if all else fails, pretend everyone is in their underwear."

"What? Ew!" I exclaimed.

He wasn't laughing, so it must not have been a joke.

"Yeah, don't you know that old trick? If you pretend everyone is in their underwear, it takes the stress off you. I used to do that when I played a big game. It worked for me every time."

The door opened, and a woman looked at us. "They're ready for you."

Mr. Fern held the door for me, and she led us to the front of the room. The chamber was intimidating. I felt like I was in court or testifying before Congress. A panel of people looked down at me from their perch. Scanning the room quickly, I saw Leah and Michael seated near the window. Mom and

Marco were in the back, and Mr. Fern took a seat in the front row. Seated directly in front of me was Superintendent Lacy. Other important-looking people filled the remaining seats. The woman gestured for me to take a seat at the front table. She adjusted the microphone and tapped on it, creating a thud that could be heard throughout the chamber.

"Thank you and welcome to today's anti-bullying presentation meeting. We will be hearing from Neepa Irving, who will present the student-led anti-bullying initiative for our consideration and approval," the superintendent announced. She then looked directly at me, smiled, and nodded, as if to say, "Please proceed."

My heart pounded so loudly that I thought the microphone would pick it up. With a deep inhale and exhale, I reached for the file that contained my notes. When I opened it, a yellow sticky note was on top. It read:

Blue jay, blue jay, how striking are you.

Basking all that see you in the vibrancy of blue.

Singing loud and proud for all to hear.

Give me confidence to express myself without fear.

I turned around to look at Mom. She blew me a kiss and mouthed, *You got this!*

"Superintendent Lacy and panel. Thank you for the opportunity to develop a district-wide anti-bullying program. Before I get into the details, I would like to acknowledge three other people who were instrumental in developing the student portion of the proposal. Leah Michaels, Michael Beekman, and Principal Fern. If you will indulge me, I would like to start off by telling you a story." Superintendent Lacy nodded her approval.

"When I was younger, my mother and I moved often, so I was always the new kid in school. I was quiet and very shy. My first instance of bullying came when I was six, the first week I started at a new school. It began off innocently enough, teasing that turned into gossiping, that eventually resulted in being pushed down on the playground, while others just watched. When I told my mom, she went to the school and filed a complaint. The bullies stopped physically hurting me, but whenever there wasn't a teacher around, they would say horrible things to me. Because I was new and shy, I didn't complain again. I thought, at least they're not hurting me. This type of behavior happened at every school I attended.

"A few years later, when I was at a school in Seattle, a group of girls pretended to be my friend. They would invite me to play and eat lunch with them; all the while, they were mean to me. It didn't happen much in the beginning, but over time, their behavior got worse. They would take my homework when I wasn't looking and step on my lunch, pretending it was an accident. From the outside, it looked like they were my friends, but in reality, they were horrible to me.

"I stopped telling my mom because bullies always find a way to get at you, and in time, I knew we would move again. This happened to me for the next ten years. When it occurred this year, I resigned myself not to say anything because nothing was done in the past, so why would I expect something to change now? My friends urged me to speak out, but I knew if I did, the bullying would escalate.

"Fortunately for me, this time was different. I realized the problem was not me. The person doing the bullying was the one unable to deal with their own issues. I saw my bully as a person no different from me, someone who had been hurt and wanted to make it stop. I tell you this story because to stop bullying, everyone needs to be on board: the one being bullied, the school, student body, parents, counselors, and law enforcement. When one is missing, the program will not work. The plan I'll present to you includes a strategy for each group that dovetails perfectly into each other. The focus of today's presentation is on the student portion, but the other elements of the plan are outlined in the previously submitted plan. Please open your packets, and I'll walk you through the details of the plan."

When I stopped to grab my packet, I looked up to see the superintendent and the other panelists leaning forward in their seats. Glancing back at Mr. Fern, he gave me a thumbs-up and a smile that was straight from the heart. *You got this, Neepa.* I continued to run through the strategy.

"Superintendent Lacy, before closing, I would like to share some wisdom from my grandfather in the form of a poem.

Tree, tree your branches are profound.

Pulling your strength from deep within the ground.

Your canopy provides protection from the storm.

Transformation and liberation now become the norm.

"We have the strength of many to make a transformation for those who are not as strong. I respectfully request that you approve this plan."

OMG, I did it, I really did it! When I pushed my chair back to stand, my knees felt a little wobbly. The superintendent rose to her feet and started clapping. The rest of the panel followed suit, as did the audience. I looked around the room, confused at first, then I saw Mom and Marco in the back, jumping up and down. Leah and Michael were hooting and hollering, and Mr. Fern gave me an enormous smile. Once the applause died down, Superintendent Lacy began.

"Neepa Irving, I was taken by you when I saw your interview on the news, and I knew you had the ability to help us create substantial change. The student plan that you, Miss Michaels, and Mr. Beekman developed is comprehensive and well thought-out. You've put us on solid footing for positive change. Thank you for your hard work, and I commend you for sharing your story. You may not know it, but speaking out gives others the strength to do so themselves. We will deliberate and have an answer in the next few weeks. Meeting adjourned."

Within seconds, Leah and Michael were by my side. We were all jumping up and down like we had just won state. "Neepa, holy shit, I didn't know that you could present like that," Leah remarked. "Oh, excuse me, sir."

"Don't worry, Leah, you said exactly what I was thinking," Mr. Fern replied with a chuckle.

"Nice job, Chicago. You really pulled that one off."

"Neepa, excuse me. Neepa." I heard Mom's voice as she worked her way through the crowd. I rushed over to hug her. "Honey, I am so . . ."

"I know, Mom, proud of me."

She whispered in my ear. "Neepa, you did an amazing job, and yes, I'm so proud."

"Thank you. I'm proud of me, too."

Marco was right there next to her. "Beautiful, smart, a model, and now a fantastic public speaker. The world is your oyster, Neepa Irving."

I blushed.

"Model? Michael questioned.

Leah nudged me and whispered, "Is that the owner of Bernardi leather?"

"Oh, Mom, Marco, these are my friends Leah and Michael."

Leah went straight for Marco, hand out. "Mr. Bernardi, I love your bags."

"Oh, ahh, thank you."

Mom broke the awkwardness. "Michael and Leah, I have heard so much about you. Thank you for being such good friends with my daughter."

Quietly, Superintendent Lacy joined our group. "Principal Fern, nice work."

"Thank you, but it was Neepa, Leah, and Michael who did the heavy lifting."

"You all should be very proud of yourselves. This was one of the most comprehensive plans I have received in my tenure as superintendent. Stressing that bullying is everyone's problem and can't be solved without everyone taking ownership is simple but brilliant. It puts the onus on the entire community. Parents can't expect the school to do something if they haven't done the work at home with their child. And the school can't expect counselors, security, and law enforcement to do their jobs well, if the school is not supporting them. You all have bright futures ahead of you. Principal Fern, we will be in touch."

The next day at school, there seemed to be a buzz. People were smiling at me and pointing as I passed. I knew they couldn't have heard about my presentation. There were no cameras in the meeting. Sitting at our usual lunch table, Enapay put down his tray.

"What is going on? Everyone is talking about you."

"I don't know."

"They saw the Bernardi Leather campaign," Leah announced as she sat down.

"What? I haven't received my copy yet," I complained.

Leah handed me the magazine just as Rebecca and Julie showed up. An enormous pink sticky marked the page. I turned to it.

"What? You look amazing," Julie shouted.

"OMG, Neepa, is that really you?"

"Damn girl, you look good. Don't hit me." Enapay cringed.

I was silent, not knowing what to do. Michael yelled at me from across the cafeteria. "Chicago, I told you, you clean up good."

All this attention, and I was still alive. Nothing bad happened. Slowly, a feeling of calm came over me. I went within myself and could feel Grandma and Grandpa with me.

"Neepa, hey, you in there?" Enapay asked.

"What?"

"People want your autograph."

"Huh. Seriously?" I laughed.

"Yup."

There was a line forming in front of our table. Enapay stood up. "Okay, everyone, single file."

"Enapay, what are you doing?" I hissed.

"Organizing your fan club," he whispered. "Should we charge?"

"Absolutely not. I thought you guys said that no one at school looked at this type of magazine."

Julie was quick to respond. "No, that was you who said it. We all knew better."

CHAPTER 21

The weather was warming up, and spring was just around the corner, hopefully. Life had been so busy, I hadn't gone to the park in forever. As soon as I entered, the weight of the world fell off me. Under my tree, I reflected.

The anti-bullying plan was presented, and the plan was approved. My first modeling gig, per Marco, was successful, and somehow I was still alive. School was winding down, and we would soon be out for summer break. Grandma and Grandpa's house sold, so now we had real money to buy our own house. Mom and Marco were going strong, and Mom was studying to take exams to become a financial planner. Soon, we would take a trip back east to spread Grandma's and Grandpa's ashes on tribal lands.

Much had happened over this past year. A lot more good than bad, and in a couple of months, I would be turning seventeen.

Before, my only goals in life had been to finish high school and not get pregnant like my mother. Now, I have dreams of so much more. I want to help people remember who they really are. To help them know that their past does not dictate their future. My wings are strong, and I am ready to fly.

"Excuse me." I heard a voice coming from the other side of the tree. I looked over to see a girl around my age.

"Yes."

"Are you Neepa Irving?"

"Uh-huh."

"I have seen you in the park often but never had the courage to say anything to you."

"Do we go to school together?"

"Yes, I'm a freshman, and I wanted to say thank you."

"For what?"

"For letting me know it's not me. I'm not the problem, and I don't deserve to be treated that way."

As she turned to walk away, I asked, "Are you okay?"

She looked back and said, "Now I am. Thank you."

I leaned back against my tree and watched the girl leave. From the corner of my eye, I saw a monarch butterfly float by. Peace filled me, and I smiled.

"Thank you, Grandma, and Grandpa. Your butterfly is quiet no more."

FROM THE AUTHOR

The Quiet Butterfly is a result of my personal struggles with the bully inside—the negative voice that creates doubt and the feeling of unworthiness. I thought, "Wow, at my age, and I am still trying to quiet that negative voice in my head? How do young people manage?"

Coupled with the growing incidents of bullying in our schools, I wanted to create a story that both young people and adults could relate to. A story that provides guidance through unlikely places that I trust will inspire and help anyone recognize their own inner strength.

Like a butterfly, we have stages in life. Some are more beautiful than others, but in the end we all can fly high. All it takes is a leap of faith.

Below is a list of resources available for students, parents, and educators to identify, respond to, and stop bullying. Stand up and speak out against bullying and remember October is National Bullying Prevention Month.

Pacer National Bullying Prevention Center provides resources and education for teachers, parents, and children.

http://www.Pacer.org/bullying/

An official website of the United States government. The U.S. Department of Health and Human Services provides resources on bullying prevention, federal laws, and what schools and children can do.

https://www.StopBullying.gov

National nonprofit organization that provides a helpchat crisis line and resources on how to get help and ways to give help.

https://www.StompOutBullying.org

Center for Disease Control and Prevention Injury and Prevention Control lists warning signs, statistics, and information on how to identify and prevent bullying.

https://www.cdc.gov/injury/features/stop-bullying/index.html

The American Academy of Child and Adolescent Psychiatry Bullying Resource Center provides resources to clinicians, families, and youth.

https://www.aacap.org/AACAP/Families_and_Youth/Resource_Centers/Bullying_Resource_Center/Home.aspx

Center for Parent Information and Resources supports parent centers who serve families of children with disabilities.

https://www.parentcenterhub.org

Cyberbullying Research Center provides resources for parents, students, educators, and clinicians, and information on current laws within the US as well as a mechanism to report cyberbullying.

https://cyberbullying.org

ACKNOWLEDGMENTS

An enormous thank you to my life partner, Will Wagner, for his unwavering support of any endeavor I embark upon. His encouragement and guidance have helped me overcome my writing obstacles, and his reminders to stop and recognize the progress I have made help me to truly appreciate this experience.

Thank you to our son, Mato Wagner. His optimism and belief that I can do whatever I set my mind to is the kick in the butt that keeps me going. His willingness to listen and thoughtful feedback remind me just how wonderful of a human being he is.

To my puppy dogs, Noepe and Shunka. They sit outside my office as I write and, without fail, remind me when it is time to take a break and play.

Thank you to my editor, Donna Mazzitelli, who believed in my story and, with compassion and grace, helped me to go deeper within myself to bring greater vulnerability to the characters.

To Shelly and Chelsea Wilhelm, Kelly and Addison Swindell, and Harper Mueller, thank you for reading the early drafts of this book. I appreciate your time and your candid feedback.

ABOUT THE AUTHOR

Victoria Wright has embarked on a journey to find her true self. In the process, she is remembering how to be whole, to look inward for guidance, and to know her truth. Her journey is full of beauty and discovery. She invites you to join her on your own journey of remembering.

Victoria is from Martha's Vineyard, Massachusetts, and is a member of the Wampanoag Tribe of Gay Head, Aquinnah. She and her family reside in Englewood, Colorado.